Top and Tails

Clare London

Three men, one love—and a passion he only ever dreamed of.

Karel Novak is content with his busy job in hotel refurbishment, enjoying the social scene in Soho, London and the company of new friends he met through working at With A Kick. All he's missing is a special man in his life. Or maybe two.

His first meeting with the mercurial pole dancer Leroy and his socially anxious partner Griff isn't impressive, but none of them can ignore the sexual spark that flares between the three men.

Their relationship builds in steps of passion, frustration, and finally love. Both Leroy and Griff have complex issues in their lives to work through, and at first Karel brings a new dynamic that both settles and supports them.

But although he loves his men, Karel gradually realises the issues are still present. His partners struggle with living individually as well as together. His heartfelt wish is for them to create a lasting bond as a trio—but that means putting others first, all too often.

And will that mean sacrificing his own joy and dreams?

All Rights Reserved

Dedication

To my Beloved Betas Sue, George, Lillian and Paul.

To those who love ice cream and romance.

Contents

Chapter 1

It had been a hell of a long time since he got laid.

Karel sighed to himself. That was surely the only explanation for his hungry fascination with the fabulous creature on stage at the Soho "Master Mac" club. A slender, muscled, smooth-skinned, black man with a ridiculously flexible body and a cheeky grin for the patrons as he hung from the pole, more gymnast than dancer. His buttocks were clenched tight, his biceps straining to hold him in place, his feet pointed in the way of a ballet master. It didn't matter that he was wearing a tee shirt and close-fitting shorts: he may as well have been stark bollock naked. Every single shadow of rib and muscle was clearly defined to anyone watching his moves.

Like Karel.

He sighed again, tore his gaze away from the dancer, and turned back to the bar. One more beer and then he was going home to his rented flat. *Just one*. There'd be something on the TV at this late hour to distract him, some old movie, some bizarre sex quiz show, another re-run of *Farscape*...

"Shit. Sorry, man." The guy who'd knocked into him gasped and grabbed his arm to stay upright. He had a firm, cool grip, surprising in this sweaty club room.

"It's okay." Rarely did anyone bump into Karel. Something about his size kept a respectfully wide berth around him: he was broad, held himself very straight-backed, and had a direct gaze that some people told him was intimidating. Well, most people who said that were just begging to be intimidated. They were rarely the sort of people he wanted to befriend, or even attract.

And yet sometimes he *wanted* to attract... but it didn't work. Notably with his temporary employer Patrick at the *With A Kick* ice cream shop. To say nothing of Patrick's assistant and now partner, Lee. Both gorgeous men, both great company, and both hot as hell. And both now out of Karel's reach since they officially became a couple. Wait, who was he kidding? He'd *never* had a chance with either—or both—of them, since they'd been dancing around each other from the moment he'd met them.

Well, that was the price of true love, right? Other people's, that was.

"You sure you're okay?" The clumsy man peered at Karel with bright eyes behind horn-rimmed glasses. He was cute, in a rather unique way. He looked younger than Karel, and was also well built, though not as firm. Slightly plump, with a trim beard, definitely bear-like. Comfy looking. *Cute.* Karel was surprised to find his body responding so instinctively. He wasn't often attracted to men of his own type.

"You look like you wanna be more drunk than you are." The guy's voice was deep, warm, riding on a chuckle. "Or are you high?"

"I'm fine. You're the one who bumped into me," Karel said, mildly enough.

The man laughed. It was a loud, uninhibited sound, so maybe *he* was drunk, but it seemed genuine. His gaze ran up and down Karel and his eyes widened with appreciation. "You're really fit. You wanna go somewhere and fuck?"

Karel blinked. He could be as blunt as the next man, but this was... *totally more so*, as Lee would say. "I like your invitation," he said, no irony intended. "But I'll pass."

"It wouldn't be until later." The man hiccupped, though he tried to hide it with a hand over his mouth. "That's my guy on the pole. Gotta wait for him to finish his set first."

Karel blinked again. A kernel of anger flared into life inside him. "Yes, I think you'd better. And then ask him what he thinks about you asking a stranger in the bar for a fuck."

The man frowned. "Shit. Did I say that aloud? All of it?"

"Yes."

"Shit," he repeated. His eyes dimmed behind the glasses. "It's not like that, you know."

It never is. Karel decided to forego his last beer and just go home. He'd been propositioned plenty of times at the club—and did some propositioning himself, because that was the way of things and no offence was meant to anyone—but there was something bizarre about this one. "Excuse me," he said, seeking the way to the exit through the crowd. *Pity.* He would have liked to spend some more time ogling the guy on the pole, whether he was taken or not.

But the clumsy guy was still up in his face. "Christ. I mean... I've been a complete arsehole, haven't I?"

What was he meant to say to that? Karel just nodded.

"Can I get you a drink? I mean, to say sorry, not to, like, try and seduce you away or anything, you know?"

Karel did know, and he didn't think a drink would settle it. The stale taste in his mouth wasn't from thirst. He gave a barely-there shake of his head and squeezed firmly past the man.

"Hey!" The call came from behind him, the apology now mixed with exasperation. "Arsehole or not, my offer still stands, right?"

A burst of raucous laughter showed what the patrons nearby thought of that.

Right. Karel didn't pause on his way out.

He wasn't a prudish kind of man, in that he was open to any and all experiences. But open relationships had caused him enough trouble in the past that he wasn't keen to be drawn into the middle of one again. There were plenty of single men to play with. He just hadn't found any he liked enough, not for a while.

He gave a final glance at the dancer. The man dipped upside down, low on the pole, his curly hair hanging down from his smooth brow and his palms open in a plea for applause. There was no mistaking his grin of pleasure and satisfaction as the room erupted in appreciation.

Karel watched the man's face until the door to the exit swung shut behind him.

Pity.

Chapter 2

"It's you! Hey!"

Karel didn't turn immediately. He was walking steadily through the quieting streets of Soho, on his way to the Tube after a long day's work at a hotel refurbishment project. The late afternoon was still bright at this time of year, the pale sun warm on his back, and he welcomed the feeling of physical work well done. Like the commuters around him, all he wanted now was to get home. He'd have a hot shower then some food, maybe a beer, followed by some TV watching and bed. He wasn't pausing from that for anything else. Besides, the voice could have been pitched at anyone, and he never assumed a call was for him unless his name was used specifically. But when a hand landed on his arm, he was startled to recognise the firm, cool grip from the club the other night.

He turned to face the glasses-guy, who looked a lot more alert today than he had before. Still cute, Karel couldn't help noticing. He was wearing a brightly coloured polo shirt, snug across his belly, and well-worn jeans that hugged his hips and arse. He carried himself well for a big man: there was no inhibition there.

And the sexy dancer boyfriend? Was standing right next to him.

"Hi," Karel said. Well, it wasn't like he claimed to be a witty conversationalist, did he? Not after a day of hard, manual work. Nor was he embarrassed by his work clothes—his comfy but worn shirt, his paint-spattered jeans—but the dancer looked fabulously fashionable in a form-fitting, thin T-shirt in some kind of metallic fabric, and skinny black jeans that showed the fine curve of his calves. Karel felt disturbingly wrong-footed.

The two men didn't seem to care what he said or wore: they both smiled at him encouragingly.

"Griff says you were at the club last Saturday," the dancer said. His voice was relaxed and light, almost musical. "He was a total arsehole to you, apparently."

Karel laughed. How could he not? "It's fine. He over-shared a little, I admit. But considering we were in a social club, it was in context."

"What a delicious accent you have. Doesn't he, Griff?"

Griff scrutinised Karel. "So where are you from?"

Karel frowned back. "Wandsworth. What about you?" And although it wasn't usually his way to make people feel uncomfortable, he watched with some satisfaction as Griff coloured.

The dancer laughed even more loudly and thrust his hand out towards Karel. "I love your style! I'm Leroy, by the way."

"Karel." Karel was surprised by the dancer's enthusiastic response, but he made himself shake Leroy's hand. It was unnerving, how much he liked the firm, sensual grip: how he didn't really want to let go. At least, not for some time.

Griff, the boyfriend, didn't offer his hand, but glanced warily between Leroy and Karel. "So, yes, I'm an arsehole. I thought we already established that."

Karel took pity on him. "It's okay, I know what you mean. I live in Wandsworth but I'm originally from the Czech Republic." He smiled at Griff. "My mother says I talk like a Londoner and should be ashamed of myself. But my British friends still find eccentricities in my speech."

"It's charming," Griff said abruptly, startling Karel. The spark of interest had returned to his very direct gaze. "And I said you were fit, didn't I?"

"You did," Karel said. Griff appeared to have filter problems, even when he was sober but, in Karel's experience, that wasn't the worst thing in the world. He turned back to Leroy, whose gaze darted up quickly from the area around Karel's mouth.

"No offence, then?" Leroy's smile hadn't wavered from its original high wattage.

"No," Karel said, and found he meant it. "None taken."

"Excellent." Leroy twisted gracefully, one hand on Griff's elbow, the other reaching for Karel's arm. "Let's go and have ice cream."

"Sorry? I'm on my way home. And I'm not dressed for socialising, I'm afraid." Karel met Griff's gaze over Leroy's shoulder.

The bespectacled man gave a wry grin. "You look pretty good to me," he said.

Leroy's eyes darted between them, his smile growing as he tugged them in the direction of *With A Kick*. "It's fine, Karel. *You're* fine. Indulge me!

Just for a while. You tried this place? It's great. Alcoholic ice creams, and I'm not just talking about a dribble of limoncello over vanilla."

Karel nodded, but Leroy continued without noticing.

"They had a fire or something, and were closed for a while. But they opened again last month and I've been itching to get back."

"It was a gas explosion," Karel said calmly.

Both Griff and Leroy turned to stare at him.

"A gas explosion," Karel repeated. "Not a fire, though there was fire damage. They are friends of mine, and I helped with the refurbishment."

"Well, well. Aren't you a dark horse?" Leroy's eyes glinted with delight. "Friend of the management! That's my favourite kind of man."

He appeared fascinated with Karel, and Karel had to admit he liked that a lot. Griff was still watching him, too, with something that looked rather obviously like hunger, and not for desserts.

Karel's heart skipped a beat.

He laughed aloud, breaking the momentary tension. "Yes, I'll join you, just for a while. But I will buy the first ices, okay?"

Lee was serving in the shop with more spirit than usual. He was a mixture of eagerness and nerves as he showed them to a table near the window, dispensing menus with pride—Lee and his friend Phiz produced witty, themed listings of the ices as often as they had time and marketing funds—and taking their order. But as he dished their ice cream into brightly-coloured bowls on the counter, he seemed unusually restless. He kept glancing towards the kitchen, and when he brought over the tray of dishes, he'd forgotten to include Karel's Ice Bergman, made with peppermint schnapps.

"Sorry. Dammit. Wait a minute, I'll fetch it."

"I can do that myself," Karel said amiably. He could see the bowl, perched on the counter behind the freezer cabinet display.

"God, no, that's my job. I should have run through the specials as well. What am I like? The Twist and Two Balls is on sale this week," he chattered on, his voice unusually brittle. "And there's a new version of Redbeard's Revenge with rhubarb vodka and ginger ale. Patrick also has a multi-scoop ice cream on the drawing board infused with the latest flavoured gins, but that's not really ready for release yet—"

"Lee, is anything wrong?" Karel broke in. When Griff, Leroy, and Lee himself stared back at him, he reckoned he'd been a little too blunt. He didn't always remember—or see the need—to waste time on small talk.

"I'm fine," Lee said quickly. Maybe too quickly. Karel had discovered that one benefit of being too blunt, and unashamed of it, was that it allowed you the opportunity to experience people's instinctive replies. "I mean, I could do a better job if I was allowed in the kitchen, but I'll just stick with being restricted to a front of house role, even though, God knows, I'm perfectly capable of coping with the ups and downs of daily work, the same as any business partner would be."

Ah. Karel knew that Lee and Patrick's business partnership was newly legalised, although they'd worked together for many years. It appeared there might still be some teething issues in play.

As if summoned by Lee's words, a tall, bearded man appeared at Lee's shoulder.

"Patrick," Karel acknowledged, smiling in welcome. "The shop is looking great nowadays."

"Thanks, Karel. It's good to see you again, and I'm always glad when you're here as a customer rather than having to work. Though, that said..."

"Yes? Do you need more help?" Karel had enjoyed working at *With A Kick*, even though the circumstances had been distressing. The shop was much loved by the Soho community, and everyone had mustered together to help out in its recovery. It had been like one of the building "SOS" TV programmes, and Karel appreciated having been welcomed into the group of friends involved. In fact, he treasured the sense of community, one he'd missed since leaving his home country. It seemed he'd withdrawn a little too much into his own company.

"We're fine," Lee said, rather mulishly. "Everything's fine. There's no risk involved anywhere."

"Risk?" Karel asked with a frown.

Patrick raised his eyebrows. "Yes, well. I know you're busy in the hotel job, Karel, but could you find some time to take a look at the kitchen cabinets? The outer wall took the brunt of the blast, and I think some of the fixings are warped."

"For God's sake, it's perfectly safe," Lee muttered gracelessly.

"Yes, perfectly safe," Patrick repeated, but with a tone that implied he had plenty of opinion to offer that wasn't necessarily in agreement with Lee's, and he wasn't being distracted from that. "At the moment, anyway. But I'm nervous of Lee working in there with the cupboards less than secure. Can you help?"

Lee rolled his eyes, but his expression softened, and he leaned into Patrick's side in a more conciliatory fashion.

Karel admitted how attractive it was, the way Patrick protected Lee. They looked so good together and acted—usually—in tandem so well. "Let me take a quick look while I'm here."

With a glance at Griff and Leroy to check they didn't think him rude to leave them, Karel stood to follow Patrick to the counter. Lee stayed with the others, his initial skittishness forgotten with the opportunity to describe some of the new ices to fresh customers. The shop was temporarily quiet with no new visitors at the counter, and Karel walked through the kitchen with Patrick, examining the fittings. One of the main wall cabinets was shaky, its moorings still in place, but knocked slightly off-kilter from the effects of the explosion. It was full of cooking pans and would very likely cause damage if it fell during working hours. Patrick was right to be concerned even if, as Karel had guessed, Lee thought it unnecessary fussing.

Karel paused in the doorway back into the shop, cleaning his hands on a tea cloth, running through a quick estimate for Patrick on re-fixing the cabinet with additional brackets.

Patrick glanced over to where Karel had been sitting. "New friends?"

Karel looked over as well. Leroy and Griff were nestled on seats next to each other on one side of the table, Lee opposite them on the seat recently vacated by Karel. Leroy's head was thrown back in a laugh at something Lee was saying. Griff leaned into Leroy, nodding, eyes shining with concentration. He had one hand under the table top, and from the relaxed angle of his shoulder and elbow, it seemed to be resting on Leroy's thigh.

Beside Karel, Patrick cleared his throat. "Sorry, I don't mean to pry."

It looked as if Lee was telling one of his funny stories about the explosion, his arms sketching a wide arc in the air, his eyes wide, his throat taut, and his mouth and cheeks wobbling as if suffering high G-forces.

"He makes a joke of it," Patrick said softly. "It's his way of getting over the shock and pain of the accident. His way of making the memories bearable for us both."

Karel had listened to some of these stories: he'd laughed, too. Everyone behaved differently in the face of shock and tragedy, a truth he'd realised from an early age. It wouldn't be right if Patrick felt uncomfortable with Lee's coping methods. "Lee tells a good tale," he said. "I think it a good strategy."

Patrick looked at him quickly, surprised, then smiled and nodded. When his gaze returned to Lee—which, in Karel's experience, it always did, every free moment Patrick had—he looked thoughtful, but reassured.

"I met those two at the club," Karel said. "Yes, they're new friends."

"I have no business quizzing you about whatever friends you have, of course. I just thought those two..." Patrick's gaze darted between Karel and the customers in question. "They look very interesting."

By now, Griff sat back with his arms crossed over his broad chest. His eyebrows were drawn in a frown, but a broad smile creased his face. Leroy wriggled in his chair, his head nudging Griff's, his dark eyes glittering with mischief. Maybe he was telling a joke in return. Maybe he was teasing him.

As Karel watched, Leroy ran a finger along Griff's jaw, tugging gently at his beard. Griff lazily swatted Leroy's hand away, still smiling. His eyelids drooped, as if he were sleepy. Or horny, maybe.

"They like you," Patrick said softly.

"Huh? We only just met."

"They're watching you. In between laughing at Lee's storytelling, sharing their own conversation, they keep looking over at you. They've been doing it since you all came in."

"Showing off." Karel laughed. He could see how Leroy and Griff bounced words and actions off each other's reactions, with an easy familiarity.

"No. Well, maybe. But they're also interested in you."

Karel shook his head. "They're watching each other. They're a couple."

"So? That doesn't mean they can't like you, too."

Karel caught Patrick's gaze. "That's not weird to you?"

Patrick laughed. "Not a lot is, Karel. I may be conservative nowadays—and sincerely monogamous—but that's not to say I didn't live a little wildly in years gone by."

"Oh yeah?" came a bright voice behind Karel. When had Lee slipped away from the table and sprung up beside them at the kitchen door?

"That's a story for another time." Patrick looked flushed, though not a little mischievous, whereas Lee looked suspiciously hungry for details.

Amused, Karel left them to it. He picked up his bowl of ice cream—overladen by an enthusiastic Lee with extra schnapps and plenty of mint leaves—and wove his way carefully back to the table. He was surprisingly relieved to escape the conversation with Patrick, afraid perhaps that it was leading him into dangerous territory.

Griff and Leroy were quiet as he sat back down and handed out the bowls. For a while, they enjoyed their desserts. When Karel reached for a napkin, Leroy was reaching at the same time and their fingers brushed together. Neither of them moved away immediately—Leroy just chuckled softly—and Karel found himself reluctant to lose the contact.

When he glanced across the table, it was Griff who was smiling at him, not Leroy.

"Karel?" A small drop of ice cream lingered on Leroy's chin, until he swiped it away with a napkin, the white paper darkening with moisture between his elegant fingers. "Tell us about yourself."

Usually, Karel was more restrained with people

he'd just met, but the combination of Leroy's gaze and Griff's smile felt for him alone. *Poor fool, me.* Was he so hungry for attention? "I have a small flat in Wandsworth, and I work in construction."

"You're a builder?"

"I can work most jobs on a building project, but I can supervise sub-contractors as well, where I'm needed." Now he was offering his CV like it was an interview. How ridiculous was that? "There's not much else to tell."

"I doubt that." This time, the touch was deliberate, as Leroy's palm brushed over the back of Karel's hand and settled there. "And what do you do for fun, when you're not working? You like clubbing?"

"Occasionally."

Leroy nodded. "It was the first time I'd seen you at Master Mac's."

"You noticed me? I know Griff did, but..." Karel was sceptical, also amused at the memory. "You were upside down on a pole, playing to your audience at the time."

Leroy's eyes widened. "And you don't believe I can notice one individual man under those circumstances? Believe me, it's a skill I've had years to develop. Of course I noticed you."

"I suppose I thought you'd be more interested in the guys dropping money onto the stage." Karel was suddenly embarrassed. "I didn't leave you any money. For the dancing? I left early."

Leroy snorted. "You left early because my arse of a boyfriend was harassing you. And it's not obligatory to tip the dancers, you know. That's more usual for the strippers."

"The tips are an important part of it." Karel knew all the club staff relied on extra money from the punters. The basic pay, such as it was, was very low. Even lower than some of the jobs Karel had done until he built his own client base. Besides... Leroy had been as good as stripped in Karel's opinion, and gorgeous with it.

"Well, yeah. That's true." Leroy grimaced. "The club pays next to nothing otherwise. But I like it."

"The dancing?"

Leroy nodded, his eyes wide with excitement now. "It's a good little stage. The boss lets you bring your own music, have rehearsal time during the day. I can develop a fine routine there."

"He's spectacular," Griff said quietly. Both he and Leroy continued to watch Karel, but Leroy's free hand reached to grasp Griff's, laid on the table top. For that brief moment, all three men were joined in touch.

"Did you always train as a dancer?" Karel asked. He didn't want this to stop, he realised. He wanted to stay at this small café table, caught up between these two unusual, very different men. He wanted Griff's intense eyes on him, Leroy's warm palm on his.

Leroy tilted his head. "Why do you ask?"

Karel laughed. He felt light-headed, as if he were young and naive again, a teenager recently arrived in London with only his passport and a pocketful of strange currency to support him. "I just wondered. Your act was so acrobatic. I thought maybe you trained as a gymnast."

Griff laughed, and nudged Leroy on the arm. "See? I told you he was fascinated by you."

"Your act," Karel said softly. "I was fascinated by your act." But he knew none of them was fooled.

"He doesn't get enough attention," Griff said, rather hotly. "They don't pay him enough, they don't give him a costume budget, they change his shifts at a moment's notice. Half the guys in the place are drunk, the rest are too focussed on hooking up with someone. I mean, not enough people watch him properly—not enough realise what work goes into his performance."

"That's me. Mr Never Enough." Leroy sighed, but he grinned at Griff. "I don't do it for world fame, man. You know that."

"I know that, for sure. Not for the money, either. You gave away half your tips last week to that bulked-up twink who does the military-theme act—"

"He's just a boy," Leroy said to Karel in an aside. "Too shy. He doesn't know how to invite the decent money yet."

"—and there's no way you'll get paid for sharing rehearsal time with that karaoke kid who couldn't drag a bag of groceries, let alone deliver a fully tarted-up dominatrix diva—"

"The kid hasn't had singing training," Leroy explained to Karel. "I just help him steady the melody. And maybe a little extra help with his make up."

Leroy's eyes were never still, even when fixed on Karel. A small starburst of light reflected there at all times, from amusement, excitement, wariness, self-deprecation—Karel didn't know for sure. Not yet.

"You're taken advantage of," Griff grumbled. He stared at Karel, as if inviting his support.

Leroy shifted on his seat, and Karel could easily see when the light in his eyes switched to irritation.

"Shut up, Griff. No one wants to hear this shit."

Karel cleared his throat. "*I* want to." What had possessed him to say that? "I want to hear about you."

"Yeah?" Griff looked angry and pleased, all at the same time. His open, expressive face could handle it, Karel thought. Leroy was more mercurial, but on a lighter level. Griff's intensity seemed to carry a whole raft of emotions.

"About both of you," Karel said. He'd never seen the point of hiding honest reaction.

Griff laughed loudly. A couple of customers at the back of the room turned briefly to look at the three men, then looked away when they just saw a guy being loud. It wasn't unusual in Soho.

Leroy tightened his hand on Karel's. He didn't seem to care about holding a man's hand in full view of the shop and passing pedestrians. Karel really liked that in him.

"I did train as a gymnast, as a boy. But by the time I reached my early teens, I knew I was never going to make it at competition level. I wasn't... well, my parents made that quite clear. There are more opportunities in dancing than in sport, if you're..." He paused. "Average, I suppose I'd call myself."

"More than that," Karel said. "Much more."

Leroy's cheeks pinked but he didn't agree with or challenge Karel's opinion.

"His mother is a ballerina," Griff added eagerly. "Only the second black woman to dance at the Royal Ballet."

Karel was impressed. That probably explained Leroy's fabulous grace and strength, also his choreographic talents. He turned to Griff. "And what about you?"

"Work, you mean?" Griff was dismissive, as if he didn't expect the same degree of interest in him. "This and that."

"He's a chef. A very fine one." There was no mistaking the pride in Leroy's voice. "He's worked at some of the best London hotels."

Griff still looked awkard; he glared at Leroy as if Leroy had exposed a hideous secret.

"That's excellent," Karel said warmly. He admired all skills, whether they were valued in the wider marketplace or not. So often, he'd discovered, they weren't, but that didn't make someone a less valuable person.

"He'll cook for you," Leroy said eagerly. "For all of us, right? Tonight. What do you say, Griff?" He turned to his partner, shifting again on his seat.

This time, he almost vibrated with joy.

Karel blinked slowly. "That's too short notice, surely."

"No way." Leroy chuckled. "Griff always has the kitchen at the flat well stocked."

Was it his place to answer for his partner? Karel wasn't sure it should be. He smiled at Griff. "I appreciate the offer, but I will come another time, when it's convenient."

Griff looked wary—did he think Karel was teasing him?—but answered readily enough. "It's fine. Seriously. Whatever."

"Aren't you working?" Karel imagined they both mainly worked nights, Leroy in the club and Griff in a hotel or restaurant.

Leroy started to speak, but Griff interrupted him, his gaze still on Karel. "I'm not working anywhere at the moment. I want you to come over." When Leroy nudged his shoulder, he still didn't break the connection, except to add, "Please."

Karel nodded. "Thank you. I will. I'd like that." He was pleased to see Griff's face light up, at the same time as he noticed a small bead of sweat on the man's temple.

"You're enjoying this?" Griff asked, gesturing at his now empty ice cream bowl. He glanced quickly at Leroy, with just a touch of panic. "You know it's my favourite flavour. But I can't make ice cream this good at home."

"No problem." Leroy shook his head gently. "We don't expect you to."

"They offer takeaway cartons," Karel added. "Any time you want it. I could bring some with me, as my contribution to the meal."

"Any time I want it? That's excellent." Griff's good humour was restored. He winked at Leroy, who grinned back at him.

For a moment more, they were silent, Karel finishing his dessert, Griff watching him peaceably, Leroy's darting gaze on anyone who entered or left the shop.

Finally, Leroy leaned forward over the table top, his hand back on Karel's. "This is fun, right?"

"This?"

"This. Us." Leroy's hand gesture was expansive, expressive. "Chatting, joking together. We enjoy life, Karel, but we can be serious too. We care as much as you do."

"About...?"

"The important things. Our lives, our loves. The world." Leroy chuckled.

"And ice cream," Griff said, and laughed with

him. He ran a finger around the inside of Leroy's bowl, sweeping up the remains of the ice. As he sucked his finger between his lips, his eyes met Karel's again, the invitation both provocative and heated. "We care about that, too."

They all laughed, and Karel felt the light-headedness return. He wanted to smile, and never stop. Looking into Leroy's eyes was like bathing in warmth, like enjoying a very special, intimate amusement. Griff's gaze was less subtle, but fiercely admiring. Karel felt both aroused and enveloped, consumed by the two of them. *Caressed.* Was this how they treated all their acquaintances?

He couldn't allow himself to believe it was all just for him.

Not yet, anyway.

Chapter 3

Their dessert finished, they left *With A Kick* together and paused outside the shop. Karel wondered how they would leave him. He didn't for a minute believe they really expected him to go home with them, on first meeting. Maybe there'd be the promise of that dinner invitation, another time? An exchange of phone numbers? Or just a chuckle from Leroy, a fierce gaze from Griff, and a "see you around"?

The reflection of the two men in the shop window was slightly distorted by the angle, but Karel found himself watching it rather than them, as if the direct sight of this couple growing so irresistible to him was too bright. Leroy stood very close to Griff, leaning slightly backwards, balancing

Griff's forward stance. They smiled into each other's face, Griff a few inches shorter, looking up at Leroy. Griff's hand rested casually at Leroy's hip; Leroy had tucked his hand into the back pocket of Griff's jeans. It tugged the baggy denim down at one side, exposing a small sliver of pale, lightly furred flesh over Griff's waistband.

Karel's skin prickled, a delicious agony awash from the top of his head to his groin, as his desire lit up from within.

When the two men kissed, it was barely there, a shared breath, a brush of lips so fleeting that only someone watching closely could imagine what lay beneath. Karel, however, saw it very clearly—both the almost-kiss and the unashamed, uninhibited sensuality that provoked the men. And when they turned to him, grinning, he realised they'd seen him watching: may even have staged it especially for him.

"Come home with us, Karel," Leroy said.

"Thank you, but I explained I'd take dinner another time."

"Not for dinner," Griff said. "Although, don't worry about starving to death, I'll feed you something."

"He needs to do that. For you," Leroy

murmured softly. "For me, too."

"But for more than that, right?" Griff persisted, though he must have known Karel would understand what was really on the menu.

In fact, Karel knew he'd never wanted anything more. Yet something held him back. He wasn't sure whether it was fear of disturbing their existing relationship or caution on his own behalf. Something about these men affected him far beyond casual, passing lust. "You have an open relationship?"

"No." Griff's reply was almost a snap.

"Sometimes we play," Leroy amended, his fingers brushing over Griff's lips as if to forestall any more misunderstandings from his partner. "There's a difference."

Karel nodded. Of course there was.

"And you, Karel?" Leroy asked.

"Me?"

"Do you have a partner? Partners? An open mind?"

"I'm single." It was a statement, not an apology. But the closeness of the other men awakened something in him that ached.

"Happy to be so?"

Karel was sure Leroy knew the temptation

they were offering to him. "I have work. Friends." He knew it wasn't really an answer, but he wasn't open to vulnerability. Not right now. "That's good enough."

Leroy shrugged. "Yes indeed. Often it is. But, still... Come home with us tonight. We want you, you must know that."

When had they moved closer? Leroy moved sinuously, his smell—some kind of sharp, citrus cologne—teasing past Karel's nostrils in a way he hadn't noticed inside the shop. Griff was on his other side, his scent still sweet with ice cream flavours and masculine sweat, his bulkier body a comforting presence, though Karel thought he detected Griff's hands shaking.

"We must go," Griff muttered, though Karel wasn't sure whether that was directed at him or Leroy. He pushed his glasses up and down his nose in a nervous gesture. "You hear me?"

"I hear you," Leroy soothed, and took a tighter grip on Karel's arm. It was proprietary, not aggressive, and Karel welcomed the touch.

Yet there *was* threat involved—emotional threat, if not physical. Karel knew it as certainly as he knew he'd be saying yes to their invitation. "Shall I collect a tub of the ice cream to bring with me?" He meant it half as a joke, but Leroy glanced at Griff, and shook his head quickly.

"No. No time. We should get back."

Karel wanted to be sure—really sure—he was welcome. He liked spontaneity but not too much haste. And if he was just a passing entertainment for them before they went elsewhere... "Are you dancing at the club tonight?"

"Not tonight," Leroy said and linked his sinuous arm into Karel's thicker one, squeezing as if to emphasise the point. "Tonight, we're all yours."

After a short Tube journey from Soho, Karel had expected to arrive at a small flat in a shared house—like his own—but they had the whole first floor of a large house off Regents Park. Karel had worked on properties in the area, for clients who were both rich and privileged, and he wouldn't have judged Leroy and Griff in that category. It wasn't any of his business, but he wondered in passing how they came to be living here. The house was shaded by a shoulder-high wall and tall bushes in the front garden, and Leroy ran along the small, gravel drive towards a set of stone steps leading up to the front door. Karel followed the two of them into a compact foyer, the decoration a little shabby and in need of refreshing, but far from seedy. Unlike some of Karel's past lodgings, there were no abandoned bicycles here, no peeling paint, no oil smears up the walls, no background aroma of stale weed.

A staircase led up off the foyer to their personal front door, and this time Griff led the way. Leroy climbed up behind Karel, maybe a little too close, because his hand brushed Karel's arse a couple of times. Leroy wasn't likely to be clumsy on his own stairs, but nor was Karel offended. They both knew what they were doing.

The flat itself was a revelation. They entered into a generous hallway: a couple of the doors were closed, but the waning sunlight shone brightly through the doorways to the other, open rooms. Pale off-white paint, clean wooden flooring, attractive rag rugs; the faint smell of furniture polish and a lingering basil and garlic cooking sauce. With more than a touch of awe, Karel eased off his boots inside the front door, following the other two men's lead. It felt right to respect the place. But padding along the corridor in his socked feet after the pair of them, he started to relax. To feel... at home.

Was it the stylish décor, or the comforting food smells? He couldn't say for certain. And it was far from a show home, despite its size and sophistication. A glance into the living room showed men's clothing slung over the arm of the sofa, a scattered newspaper on the floor, various games consoles, beer bottles, and used water glasses on the low table.

But the kitchen was really magnificent. It wasn't a huge room, but it had enough space for a slim breakfast bar on one side, a large fridge freezer, and a marble-topped counter stocked with a dizzying array of equipment and gadgets. Karel wondered if the fittings had been Griff's doing. As Leroy fetched beers for them all from the fridge, Griff moved around the room with fresh confidence, as if he was back in his preferred domain. He no longer shook—his face took on a calmer expression. He bustled happily, collecting food ingredients, reaching for pans and utensils to whip them up a light tortilla for supper. Each time he used something from the counter or a cupboard, he would move it carefully back into place. If he spilled a drop of oil, or a splash of water from washing the side salad, he would clear it up at once.

Karel and Leroy sat side by side at the breakfast bar, chatting about *With A Kick*, the club, their music tastes, the books Leroy had read recently. Karel would read the occasional biography or non-fiction book, but he couldn't compete with Leroy, who appeared to know every book on the fiction bestseller lists, whatever the genre, even when he admitted he hadn't read all of them yet.

Karel wondered when Leroy got the time for even a fraction. His own leisure time was usually spent in watching TV, emailing his family, and preparing quotes for his clients. He'd go to the club now and then, visit a pub with a friend for a few beers. Catch up on the latest movie if one of his mates invited him along. Other hobbies... well. There had been other things, in the past. Nowadays, he rarely had the time.

It was a pleasant change in routine this evening, sitting on the surprisingly comfortable bar stool, nursing a cold, refreshing beer, occasionally passing Griff a plate or spoon as he cooked, enjoying the casual way Leroy bumped hips with him every now and then as he swivelled on his own stool with alarming carelessness. And yet... when Leroy's shoulder touched Karel's and stayed close,

Karel thought maybe it wasn't carelessness at all.

Instead, he recognised it as a dance of sorts: a dance of seduction. Griff's busy domesticity, Leroy's witty charm, the good beer, the comfort and luxury of the setting.

When the food came, they ate it with enthusiasm and pleasure. Karel hadn't realised how hungry he was, but the food on the hotel site where he was working was very basic and he'd more or less skipped lunch. Griff had infused the tortilla with herbs and chopped chillies, and the sweetest caramelised shallots Karel had ever tasted. They drank more beer, though Karel noticed how Leroy didn't pass more than a couple to Griff. They all slipped into more easy gossip about Soho's shops and pubs. Leroy and Griff seemed to spend most of their social life there—at least, Leroy did. From what Karel could deduce, Griff didn't always go with him, to the club or elsewhere. Yet they finished each other's stories, and laughed at similar memories, so they obviously shared everything regardless.

At one point—when food was almost finished, and they were sharing anecdotes about some of the more outrageous characters they'd met at Master Mac's—Griff mentioned an upcoming arts festival to be held in the area. Karel had heard Patrick talking about it, too. Most of the businesses around Soho were looking forward to the extra footfall, to say nothing of the actual acts on show.

"I had the brochure somewhere," Leroy said aimlessly. "Says what's on, and where." He didn't get up from his stool to go looking for it.

"They're using the club?" Karel asked.

Griff nodded. "Yes. Master Mac's for some daytime acts, and the comedy club too. But there are activities in the stores, too, and the church halls. And some of the hotels are hosting performances and readings."

Karel grimaced. "A pity the hotel where I'm working won't have finished its refurbishment. Maybe next year they'll take part, if it becomes an annual event."

"Here it is," Griff announced, waving a small booklet. He'd opened a shallow drawer by the cooker and extracted it from a pile of other leaflets in there. Karel could see they'd been stacked very neatly, in decreasing order of size.

Leroy shrugged. "Knew I left it somewhere."

"Lazy," Griff muttered.

"Anal," Leroy muttered back. Then they grinned at each other.

"Will there be dance shows?" Karel asked Leroy. "You'll want to watch them."

"Or take part," Griff said loudly.

There was a sudden, inexplicably tense pause. Then, "No way," Leroy said sharply. His hand had clenched by his side. "Plenty of other things to watch."

Karel saw the quick, angry glare between the two men. Leroy obviously didn't want to pursue the subject, but now Karel wasn't sure how to divert the conversation without it becoming awkward. Their bond seemed very secure, but volatile, and he had no idea how to handle it. Griff stepped into the breach, though maybe not to Karel's comfort.

"What's *your* favourite art medium, Karel?"

"Me?" Karel's heart gave a sudden, joyful jump, like a pet dog keen to be let off its lead. He took a calming breath before replying, determined to avoid anything provocative. "I like movies. Street theatre. Music, of course, though fairly middle of the road stuff. And watching dance." He smiled at Leroy.

Leroy stretched out a hand and rested his warm palm on Karel's arm.

"Leroy loves to perform," Griff said.

"I know that," Karel said softly, his eyes on the

sinews along Leroy's long, wiry arm. "I've watched him."

Leroy smirked. "Yeah. I can dance there four nights a week, if I'm lucky."

"Do you only dance at—?"

"Club dancing suits my level just fine," Leroy continued as if Karel hadn't started a question.

In the background, Griff made a small, snorting noise. "Leroy has always wanted to teach," he said, again out of the blue. "Thinks dance is a way to keep kids off the street. Teaches them ways of expressing themselves."

Leroy flushed, but lifted his chin proudly. "And I'm right, aren't I?"

"It saved *you*," Griff said, then dropped his voice to a gentler tone. "At least, it mostly did."

"If you need my opinion," Karel said. "I agree, too. There are too few opportunities for art, at school and beyond. And not enough facilities." He thought not only of Leroy's dancing talent, but his vivacity, his easy speech, his innate charm. "I think you'd be very good at teaching."

"I like exhibition art, especially installations," Griff continued blithely.

Karel, still thinking about and imagining Leroy dancing, was caught unprepared for the change of subject. He stilled, praying his expression didn't give anything away.

"Like the pile of bricks? The unmade bed?" Leroy said, almost a sneer.

"Who's to say that doesn't have a message for some people?" Griff fired back. It seemed to be a familiar argument. Griff nodded at Karel, maybe looking for support. "Leroy doesn't have much feeling for things that don't move. But I like sculpture, too. Something that's three dimensional, that has construction behind it. A physical creation. Someone has to twist materials, hammer them home, chip away at stone."

Karel needed to stop this conversation. Not that the guys weren't perfectly entitled to talk about whatever they chose, in their own home. But he didn't want to get drawn into—

"There are several sculpture exhibitions, one at the local school." Griff opened the booklet, as if ready to search the index.

"Karel?" Leroy was looking at him curiously. His hand squeezed Karel's, his thumb distracting, massaging Karel's wrist. He threw a comment to Griff, over his shoulder. "Let's talk about something else."

"Huh?"

Leroy rolled his eyes. "Man, it's too late tonight for chatting about art and stuff. Isn't it?" The question was aimed at Karel.

"I... don't mind," he said.

But Leroy laughed. He swept the brochure from Griff's hand, dropped it on the far end of the counter, then turned fully to face Karel. "Yeah. Talk about something else, Griff. Something just for fun. Like the time you made chilli frozen yoghurt and burned my mouth at the same time my tongue froze to my teeth—"

"—or the time you bought kids' dance tights by mistake, fell over trying to put them on, and nearly strangled your balls?" Griff countered.

Everyone laughed. The awkward moment had passed. Karel was relieved he hadn't been led astray by his own worries. The kitchen was suddenly full again of amused banter, with Griff leaning over the counter to gossip, and Leroy's soothing yet stimulating touch on Karel's skin.

And underlying all of it, a thread of fizzing, humming desire growing between them. Karel wondered how he would have coped if the conversation had gone a more cultural route, when all he could think about at the moment was energetic, obscene sex with these men.

He didn't think he was presuming anything, either.

Finally, Leroy collected their empty plates, placed them in the dishwasher, then sauntered back to where Karel sat. He didn't sit back down again, but stood there, his hip nudging Karel's. Griff wiped the counter briskly but thoroughly with a wet cloth, placed it neatly on the side of the sink, took off his glasses, then came to stand beside him.

The dance was moving into its second set.

Karel stood, as steadily as he could. His skin prickled as if electricity sparkled over it, and his limbs felt almost too weak to respond. But when Leroy leaned in to kiss him, he was more than ready. He cupped Leroy's cheek, thumbing the gentle bed of stubble, enjoying the brush of Leroy's hair on the back of his hand. Karel pushed his tongue gently at Leroy's mouth and the lips parted quickly, eagerly, for him. They kissed in near silence, the only sound their panting, the soft slick of their mouths.

And Griff's soft breath in Karel's other ear. "We've taken this evening in the wrong order," he said.

When Karel turned reluctantly from Leroy's kiss, he found Griff staring at him with a slow, seductive smile that Karel hadn't seen before.

"Dessert before the main course," Griff explained with a wink.

"No," Leroy said with obvious amusement in his voice. "That was only ice cream. The proper dessert hasn't even been served yet."

"Whatever," Griff murmured, rolling his eyes like Leroy had earlier, still smiling at Karel. He lifted his face for a kiss. His lips were plumper, his mouth wider. Karel didn't know why he should be shocked that Griff's taste was so different, but he was delighted by it. Griff was surprisingly assertive, thrusting his tongue into Karel's mouth, his beard softly tickling Karel's chin.

Leroy hadn't moved away. His breath was warm on Karel's neck, but Karel appreciated the way Leroy took his time: no one was hurrying. He relaxed into Griff's kiss as he had Leroy's, and behind him, Leroy's lips touched the nape of his neck, kissing around to Karel's throat and down towards his collarbone. Griff nipped briefly at Karel's lower lip and Karel gasped with pleasure. Leroy slid his fingers briefly, tantalisingly, under the neck of Karel's T-shirt, running along the seam, tugging it away from his body.

"I worked on the site today," Karel said, not

surprised to find his voice was hoarse. "I'm sweaty. My clothes are dusty."

"You can shower here," Griff said quickly. "If you want. Or…"

"…No. Do it after," Leroy said, just as quick. His tone roughened. "I want you like this."

Jesus. A wave of desire swamped Karel from head to foot. He leaned away from Griff as Leroy shifted his grip to the bottom of Karel's T-shirt and peeled it over Karel's head.

Griff's gaze dropped to Karel's chest and he licked his lips.

Leroy sighed happily. Then he took Karel's hand and led him out of the kitchen.

Chapter 4

Karel had never seen such a big damned bed. The rooms in the flat were generous, but even so, the guys' bed left little space between its edges and the walls. It must have been specially made because it seemed longer and wider than any kingsize Karel had ever seen. The mattress was thick, the plump duvet was covered in a stylish pale grey and black fabric, and a selection of pillows were bundled up against the headboard. They must have their clothes stored somewhere else because there were no wardrobes, though maybe two of the rooms on this outer side of the building could have a walk-through built in—

And what the hell was he doing, thinking construction issues when he was in a bedroom, half naked, with two gorgeous men?

Leroy struggled with his skinny jeans as they snagged around his muscled calves. Laughing, Griff crouched to help him pull them off. The top of Griff's buttocks showed over the drooping waistband of his jeans. Smooth skin, a light but extensive layering of hair, generous flesh. Karel wanted—desperately—to touch.

When Griff pulled off his polo shirt and dropped his jeans, Karel's mouth went dry. Sexual excitement thickened the air in the room. They were choreographing this, he was sure, though who could blame them? They both had so much to show off. After Griff got naked, Leroy took his turn, peeling off his mesh vest and briefs. All they had to do was yank off socks, and they were nude.

Karel didn't have much time to admire, let alone touch, before they closed in on him, a very willing prey, crowding him against the end of the bed. Leroy's nimble hands unfastened Karel's jeans, and he slipped his fingers into Karel's briefs, while Griff kissed him. Again and again, his tongue thrusting into Karel's mouth, teeth nipping at his lips. Karel's jeans and underwear dropped to the floor and instinctively he stepped out of them. The back of his legs knocked against the mattress as the other two pressed even closer.

They messed about for a while, kissing, touching, teasing. Leroy laughed a lot, whereas Griff growled and grunted in what sounded like frustration. Yet neither of them pushed the action further or faster than it seemed to need. Karel just enjoyed the astonishing pleasure of contrasting stimulation from two bodies. His hands itched to hold both the soft, hairy flesh and the taut, smooth skin, and he didn't really know where to start. How much time would he be allowed, in order to savour this experience? How did they want things to progress? It was like a dessert of many flavours: each part delicious on its own, but gorgeous combined, and leaving the customer with the agonising decision of which combination of taste to pursue next.

Although there was no specific signal, it suddenly became more serious.

Griff broke away from the kisses and stepped back, his erect cock poking Karel's thigh. Placing a hand on Karel's chest, he pushed firmly. With a choked laugh, Karel tumbled back, landing naked on the cool, fresh duvet cover, and he scooted up to the middle of the bed. Griff followed and they resumed kissing, Griff clutching him close, chest to chest, thighs to thighs. Karel could feel Griff's pulse racing against his skin; he winced with anguished need every time Griff's cock slid against his own. Then Griff rolled him flat again but didn't follow. Instead, Karel felt Leroy's hands on his knees as he parted Karel's legs.

Karel was a tall guy and he was used to his feet hanging off the end of a bed, but this one was so large, he was still fully cushioned on the mattress. He looked up into Leroy's heated gaze, drank in the sight of Leroy's strong shoulders and his torso flexing as he knelt on the bed between Karel's legs. The next second, Karel was gazing instead at the top of Leroy's head, as Leroy's mouth slid slowly and wetly over his cock.

"Shit!" Karel hadn't meant to shout, but the sensation was so *good*, and shocking in the very best way. Leroy chuckled, the sound muffled but sending small ripples of vibration all the way up Karel's shaft. His hand cupped Karel's balls, patting the taint with one extended finger as he sucked. His flexibility allowed him to bend almost in half, his chest resting on the top of his thighs, but it didn't seem to cause him any discomfort. His blowjob was very enthusiastic but controlled, too, and Karel barely had to thrust to get the right friction.

"Getting close!" he groaned. The mischievous foreplay had undermined any suspense he'd hoped to maintain. After a particularly deep, delicious stroke, he gripped Leroy's hair with one hand and flung the other arm across the bed to anchor himself.

He found Griff instead.

Griff had shifted around, still lying on his side, but now the opposite way up to Karel. His head nestled on Karel's thigh, his chin nudged Leroy's waist, and his kisses were now lavished wherever he could touch the bowed body with his mouth. All Karel could reach was Griff's knee and thigh, but as he caressed the warm skin there, he felt a clear shiver of excitement through Griff's body. After a few clumsy squeezes, Karel slid his hand between Griff's thighs to pet Griff's balls. Gasping, Griff lifted his leg to give Karel better access. He still nuzzled his kisses into Leroy's body, but when Karel curled his fingers around Griff's cock, Griff started to thrust back into Karel's fist.

They lay on the bed in a tangled, panting, distorted triangle formation. Karel was flat on his back, a hand tangled in Leroy's hair and his climax racing impatiently towards eruption. Leroy knelt low between his knees, sucking him off, and Griff rocked beside them both, thrusting in and out of Karel's grasp. It was clumsy, awkward. The bed creaked, the duvet rucked up beneath them, and Griff grunted whenever he knocked his nose against Leroy's sharp hipbone. Karel lost hold of Griff's cock—slippery now with pre-cum and sweat—a couple of times. Yes, very awkward to pleasure three, recently met, men at once.

But it was the most magnificent thing Karel had ever experienced in a bedroom.

Leroy groaned suddenly and slid Karel out of his mouth. He stretched up, arms wide, and leaned back on his heels. He looked like a wicked, wet-lipped cat and Karel's aching dick shifted on his belly with appreciation.

"Are you okay?" Karel asked. He had to clear his throat twice to get the words out.

Leroy smiled and nodded. "Never better. It's just my back, it cricks sometimes. But I'm fine. You taste so good." He pushed his hair off his sweaty forehead and beckoned to Griff. "Come try him, Griff."

But when Griff tried to shimmy down the bed to join Leroy at Karel's groin, Karel surrendered to mischief of his own. He tightened his hand around Griff's cock, effectively keeping him in place. Griff moaned softly: his dick swelled even more against Karel's palm, and he stilled, completely submissive to Karel's instruction.

Karel let go, but only for a moment. He shifted away from Leroy, and rolled onto his side, facing Griff, top to toe in the classic sixty nine position. Then he grasped Griff's cock yet again, and this time guided it deeply into his mouth.

"Jesus!" Griff yelped. "Leroy? This is way better."

Karel smiled to himself. His own cock felt hot and graceless, pressed to his belly, but he reckoned he could still give good head. Leroy had left him too close for comfort but he knew he'd get to come soon. Maybe, in the meantime, he'd payback some of that discomfort to Griff.

Another dip on the bed announced that Leroy was moving too, coming to kneel behind Karel. Karel glanced back, just once, and caught the excited sparkle in Leroy's eyes as he leaned over Karel's shoulder, watching him feast on Griff. Karel concentrated back on Griff, loving the shudders Griff gave, and the growls from the back of his throat.

"So good. *So* good," Leroy whispered in Karel's ear. He slid down to lie on the mattress, pressed against Karel's back. His nipples pebbled against

Karel's shoulder-blades, his dick was squashed against Karel's buttocks. Like that lazy cat he'd resembled, he started to rub himself sensuously against Karel.

Griff blew out a heavy breath and peered back up the bed at Karel, his eyelids drooping, his lashes wet. "Can we wait?"

"For me?" Karel smiled, his voice muffled around Griff's cock. "Or you?" He knew his own pace, and maybe they all needed to take the edge off with a blowjob, if they were going to play all night—

Abruptly, Leroy's hand grabbed him by the ear and pulled his head completely up off Griff's cock.

"Huh?" Karel was momentarily confused.

"Listen to him," Leroy whispered, his voice sly, the edge of it shaking with need.

"Me. In me," Griff growled to Karel. His hips jerked on the covers, his arms thrown wide open, the fingers furling and unfurling. "Want you to fuck me."

Karel's heartbeat sped up. "Come up here then."

Griff wriggled around quickly to face Karel. They shared another couple of sloppy kisses, then Karel pushed Griff onto his back and shuffled into the harbour of Griff's groin. It was an echo of

Leroy's earlier position with Karel, but this time it wasn't just to suck. Karel leaned down over Griff, supporting himself on his elbows, kissing Griff's mouth, his bearded jaw, his ear lobe, his neck. Griff wriggled like a landed fish underneath him, his skin hot and soft, his belly rubbing on Karel's, his thighs stretching wider apart around Karel's body, his hips canting up so their cocks nudged together, again and again. Karel's arousal spiked to full pitch. He had no idea how long he'd last before spilling at the least direct touch: it was almost too bloody painful.

Behind him, he heard a drawer being opened, then slammed shut again. A handful of foil wrappers rained down on the covers, and Leroy slid an opened condom packet into his hand. Karel was poised to take Griff, to slide into his arse. But at the same time, Leroy was with him in everything he did, the man's cologne in his nose, and his gasps creating a background soundtrack to all that was happening. *Limbs everywhere.* Leroy reached an arm between them, his palm glistening with lube. He ran his hand under Karel's cock, under Griff's furry balls, and pressed his fingers up into Griff.

"Fuck!" Griff arched up, moaning, his cock leaving a silver trail of pre-cum on Karel's belly and Leroy's forearm.

Karel moaned too. His back ached at the base of his spine, partly from stretching out over Griff, partly from the agonising tension as his dick longed for release. Leroy laughed, gripping Karel's shoulder with his free hand, holding him in place while he probed inside Griff. Then he slid out his fingers, and helped Karel roll on the condom, liberally wiping the lube along his shaft.

"Hurry!" Griff gave a snort of frustration and hooked his hands behind his knees to give better access. Karel had never known men so confident in what they wanted from him, and it was a special kind of thrill. He lined up carefully and nudged into Griff. Griff wriggled once, as if to seat Karel more comfortably inside, then tightened his muscles around him.

Karel gasped loudly.

Leroy's chuckle was strained. Karel could barely concentrate on anything other than Griff's tense channel, but he recognised the slicking sounds of Leroy jerking off, on his knees beside them. Karel started to rock in and out of Griff, their breathing matching a harsh rhythm. It was marvellous, it was mind-blowing. No, dammit, he probably *couldn't* wait—

A hand squeezed his shoulder.

"Hey." Leroy's voice was so much lower than usual, Karel barely recognised it. "My turn."

Karel stared, until he realised that Leroy meant he wanted Karel to fuck *him* now.

Both of them.

Karel could hardly breathe for the excitement. He slid carefully out of Griff: he'd felt lodged so deep it took an effort. And Griff made various complaining snuffles as if he might put up more of a fight. But Leroy had dropped his head to his arms, flat on a pillow, his arse up high. Karel quoted the Borg to himself: Resistance was futile.

He slid off the condom and fumbled with a tissue to dispose of it. Then there was the issue of pulling on another. Leroy had scattered a pile of assorted ones on the bed, and they obviously used them as toys as well as necessity. Karel could have had his choice of any colour, any surface, any taste, for that matter. He would have been amused, if he cared anything about choice at this very instant.

This time it was Griff who helped him, scrambling up to Karel's side. His face was red from their exertions, but he moved swiftly to roll on and lube Karel in turn. "We can go all night, switching like this."

Karel gave a soft yelp as Griff snapped the

condom fully tight.

"Sorry. You're close, right?" Then he looked straight into Karel's eyes and flushed. "That going all night thing? I don't think it's gonna work with you."

"I'll do my best—" Karel began his protest.

"No, it's not you." Griff caught Karel's mouth with a fierce kiss, full of tongue. "We're too close as well. We want you too much."

He guided Karel to crouch behind Leroy, to slide into his lubed hole, to settle Karel's groin up against Leroy's cheeks. The body beneath Karel this time was tight-skinned, the muscles graceful, the movements sharper and sleeker as they moved together. Leroy had lifted one hand and was still jerking himself off. He flowed in one graceful, undulating movement, like his dances, and Karel followed him blindly. He briefly, breathlessly, wondered which one of them was actually directing their sex. Leroy was quicksilver underneath him, sliding, arching. They were like one body, and moving faster in tandem. But Karel had barely worked up a new sweat when Leroy cried out, coming hard, gasping, moaning, laughing, twisting under Karel.

Laughing? Karel was enchanted. He'd never had

a lover who'd laughed in the middle of climax. He paused, Leroy tightening on him and making it difficult to move inside. All Karel wanted was to sink back into the channel, thrust the few more times he knew it would take for him to get there, too—

"Don't you dare! Me again, now."

Griff tugged hard at his arm. Turning awkwardly, Karel eased himself out of Leroy, and let himself be pulled back down on top of Griff. A muscle in his upper thigh twitched painfully, and for a fleeting, hysterical moment, he wondered if he should rejoin the local gym, and soon. But he slid into place with Griff as if he'd been made naturally for it. Griff's legs opened and lifted again around Karel, his heels scuffing at Karel's back, seeking purchase.

"A condom...?" Karel gasped. The one he'd used in Leroy had slipped off in the move.

"Can't wait." Griff wriggled so that their cocks lined up, rubbing together, damp and hot. He gripped Karel by the arms, even more tightly. "Do it this way."

Karel was speechless, his vision misting with the tension. They pitched together, increasingly frantic, slipping in the sweat on their bodies. Karel slid his hands under Griff's arse and gripped hard, trying to force him to move in the same rhythm. For one blissful moment, Griff stopped flailing and arched against Karel. They thrust, their cocks squeezed between their bellies, the friction both agonising and ecstatic.

Perfect.

And then Karel felt Leroy's arms slip around his waist from behind.

"Jesus, you look like gods," Leroy moaned. He laid his head on Karel's shoulder and rocked against him, matching the movement against Griff.

It was the final, spectacular straw. Karel knew his climax was unstoppable now. Not with two men's scent on his skin, two men's pulses close to his own, two voices moaning in his ear.

"Now." Griff's voice was somewhere between a grunt and a whisper. His fingers tightened, and he arched himself up against Karel. "Now we can all come." The last word was muffled as he gave a strangled cry, his whole body jerking. Karel felt sticky warmth on his belly and smelled the tang of seed. Behind him, Leroy gave a series of soft gasps and jerked against the small of Karel's back. Warmth hit Karel there, too, a viscous trail trickling down his skin towards his buttocks.

It had taken a Herculean effort to wait for his own satisfaction, though not as bad as Karel had thought at first—he'd been so concentrated on his two lovers, his own climax had been held at bay. But now he let loose.

One single, inarticulate cry and he joined them, completion shuddering through him like an aftershock, warming him from his groin to his toes, bringing a lump to his throat with astonished emotion, and robbing his limbs of basic strength.

And then he collapsed beside them both on that beautiful, luxurious, *big* bed.

Chapter 5

Early morning. Unfamiliar light from a bedroom window spiked across Karel's face, as his eyes took time to open properly, and he remembered where he'd spent the night. When he shifted, he winced. His muscles ached like hell.

He rolled over in bed to find only Leroy beside him. The man was curled up like a child, with his knees drawn to his chest and his hands clasped under his head like a cushion. The duvet was kicked to one side of the mattress: they'd been too hot together last night to need it. Karel ran a gentle finger down Leroy's bare thigh, reminding his senses of what they'd done the previous evening. How Leroy's body had felt under Karel's touch, how his dark skin had smelled, how his muscles had worked so hard, how his voice had laughed in the middle of orgasm, breathless and teasing.

How possessive Leroy's arse had felt, clenched around Karel's cock.

He took another few moments to savour the mix of colours, smells, and textures in this different bedroom. It was something he liked to do, wherever he was. He analysed the shapes created by the morning light on the pillows; his gaze lingered on the bold contrast of Leroy's black briefs against the white, crumpled sheets; he compared the feel of cotton bedding under his fingertips to the single drop of sweat nestling in the small of Leroy's back.

Karel finally slid off the bed without waking Leroy and washed up quietly in the guys' bathroom along the corridor. He'd taken a quick shower there at some stage during the night, despite their reluctance to let him go—he didn't like to sleep in the work day's mess. Now he padded in his boxers and yesterday's shirt to the kitchen.

Griff was already there, bare-chested, bare-footed, and wearing loose sweat pants. His glasses were perched on the very end of his nose and he was making tea. There was also a basket of bread on the counter that smelled fabulous and looked suspiciously homemade. Karel was more used to processed, same-size slices for his quick breakfast of toast and marmalade.

Griff smiled at him in that fierce, concentrated way he had, then poured Karel a large mugful of tea.

"Thanks," Karel said. Such an inadequate word to cover everything that had happened to him over the last twenty four hours, from work, to dinner, to sex, to sleep in a strange bed, to a fine cup of tea. Yet it was sincerely meant.

"Back atcha," Griff said, and hitched himself up onto one of the bar stools.

For a while, they drank their tea side by side in peace. Griff buttered a couple of slices of bread and slathered them in a dark red jam that may have been cherry, though it had other flavours of raspberry and blueberry. They ate happily, hungrily.

Despite the domestic setting, Karel was as vividly aware of this man as he had been of Leroy in the bed. He'd spent the night with them both, fucked them, cuddled with them, slept with them. This morning, Griff's body smelled of freshly washed skin and hair, yet not so scrubbed that Karel couldn't identify the notes of sweat and seed that must have drenched them in the sheets last night. As Griff reached for more jam, Karel watched, fascinated, the play of muscles across Griff's chest, the gentle ripple of flesh across his belly. Karel knew how well Griff's arse fit in his grip, how Griff knew exactly when to kiss and when to bite with that rich mouth. How Griff's rounded thighs felt, clenched around Karel's hips: how he'd bucked under Karel, how damned difficult it had been to hold back climax when Griff was all but dragging it out of him. As, in fact, both Griff and Leroy had done last night.

Several times.

That was what Karel remembered most of all—not the actual, consuming, poignant burst of climax, but the clasp of both men combined, surrounding and captivating Karel's whole body.

"Are you lonely?" Griff asked suddenly.

Karel swallowed another mouthful of tea before he answered such an abrupt question. "I'm alone. It's not the same."

"Do you have family in this country? I mean, I know you've been in England for many years. But before that?"

"My sister is here, but my parents are still in the Czech Republic." Karel had come to the city fifteen years ago, on his own, when he was barely out of his teens. He'd come with his parents' blessing, because his sister was already in London and he'd nagged them for months to let him follow her. The spirit of adventure had a strong call at that tender young age. But she had a highly paid job in financial recruitment, working long hours, and had very little spare time for him. Despite that, she'd been thrilled to see him, and insisted he stay at her flat. For almost four years he roamed most of London during daylight hours, learning his way around, improving his English to a high standard, and finding temporary jobs until he had enough money to move out on his own. His small flat in Wandsworth was cramped, but well placed for central London.

His favourite place to work and play had always been Soho, partly because of the buzz and the opportunity for jobs, but also because of the rich mix of people and nationalities. He was nothing particularly special among such cosmopolitan settings, and that suited him fine. He'd been expected to pursue his studies in England, but somehow, over the years since he arrived... he had drifted into a more casual life.

He'd always thought that also suited him fine.

Now Griff was poking him to think more closely about it. And when he sat there silently for another minute, Griff *did* poke him, physically, with the handle of his mug.

"Hey," Karel protested mildly. "I'm used to my own company. I'm not lonely." He wasn't sure if repeating it made him more or less credible.

Griff raised his eyebrows as if he wanted to take that further, but perhaps surprisingly, he let it drop.

Karel took more bread from the basket: it was excellent, thickly sliced and very tasty. "How long have you and Leroy been together?"

"Years," Griff said. "And thank the fuck for it. I'm not much good on my own."

Karel's buttocks and thighs were still stiff from last night's exercise, but every time Griff brushed a bread crumb off his hairy chest, Karel wanted to reach over and do it for him—run his fingers through the hair, and flick the nipple until it peaked to the point of discomfort. His skin goosebumped with anticipation. It was madness to want sex again so soon, after so much. He was a lunatic. *And glad of it.* He felt awake in a whole new way this morning.

"It's not everything," Griff said, abrupt again. "Being with one man. Monogamy. It has its down sides, too. A loneliness of its own, restricted to just one outlet, just one man's company. One man's understanding—one man's familiarity."

Karel frowned, a little confused. "You're not happy with Leroy?"

Griff laughed loudly and obviously genuinely, pushing his glasses farther up his nose. "Shit, no! Gotta love him. Always have done. We're together, all right."

"But you find it restrictive?"

"It's not that. I say things badly." Griff frowned as if trying to work out the best way to phrase it. "We get in a rut. We know each other *too* well. You know? Can't always see what's best, when you're too deep in to start with. And with just two... there's no perspective."

Karel thought Griff actually said things very well, but not necessarily things that should be said, or shared, in the first place. "You look after each other," he said simply.

"Yeah. Of course. That's my life!"

Karel was unprepared for the sudden flush of colour on Griff's neck, his obvious protest and pride in caring for Leroy. It wasn't something Karel understood easily. He'd always looked after himself, at least as an adult. But looking at the determined, possessive set of Griff's jaw, a feeling twisted inside his chest, almost like pain.

"And I've got nothing else to do, have I?" Griff added.

Karel tilted his head, unsure what to say. The conversation had shifted again. "You're not working at the moment, you said...?"

"Not working now, not worked for years. I can't hold down a bloody job." Griff's face twisted with sudden anguish. "You might say I don't have the corporate approach."

Karel could believe it. He'd seen Griff set to work in the kitchen and he wasn't workshy by any means. But the way he spoke so bluntly, so awkwardly, without any regard for how he'd be perceived? Karel suspected that could often be misconstrued.

Griff peered at him. "Your job suits you, right? I mean, you're good at it. People can relate to you."

"That's the same for you, I'm sure—"

"Don't patronise me!" Griff snapped.

Karel fell silent. He wasn't afraid of Griff's anger—he knew he could look after himself—but he didn't want to provoke him further, and it upset him after they'd had such a good time. Yet, what did he really know about this apparently complex man?

"Just thought that might be why you're on your own... why you came back with us last night." Griff was continuing the conversation from earlier, as if he'd never raised his voice. "Looking for something beyond that single tie."

"Now you're overstepping." Karel really didn't want to get angry in return, but things were still raw between them, and this emotional probing without any context was disturbing. "It's not your business. I'll choose my own way, thank you."

Griff didn't apologise, or maybe didn't have time to. At that moment, Leroy stepped into the kitchen doorway, wearing tight black briefs and a short robe that barely skimmed his slender, muscular thighs. He hadn't bothered fastening it, either, and one side had slipped down off his shoulder. The half-clothed look was sexier than if he'd appeared totally naked.

He haphazardly ran his hand through his hair, yawned widely, and sauntered over to them. "Morning, man. *Men.*"

And just like that, the tension between Karel and Griff lifted, and it seemed perfectly natural for them both to draw Leroy in—to surround him with a hug and caress from both sides. Griff nuzzled his neck, his arm snaking around Leroy's waist. Karel pressed a kiss to his temple, then slid his own arm around Leroy's wiry torso, capturing Griff's upper body where it pressed close. They leaned in to each other, a threesome of bodies, breath shallow, lips touching skin, fingers tightening on flesh, knees nudging between legs until someone moaned aloud with need.

Karel knew it was him. He couldn't remember the last time he'd made that sound. *Maybe last night.*

"Here's a hungry man," Leroy murmured in Karel's ear. "And not for Griff's orgasmic bread recipe." His voice was thick, not just with sleepiness, and Karel reckoned the hand caressing his thigh was Leroy's. Whereas the hand cupping his balls inside his boxers had Griff's rougher signature to it. "Do you have to work today, Karel?"

Karel was expected at the hotel, but he was a self-employed contractor: he could arrange his own schedule. He wouldn't leave the client in the lurch, but there were a couple of younger men working with him on the job, and he reckoned he could rely on them to carry the morning at the very least. "No," he said. "Not yet." He turned his head and caught Leroy's lips with his own. Leroy's tongue darted quickly, fiercely into Karel's mouth.

"Hey," Griff muttered sulkily. "Don't forget me."

Leroy just laughed softly: his breath was warm and damp on Karel's chin. He made no attempt to surrender Karel's mouth and, to be honest, Karel didn't want him to.

They weren't going to make it back to the bedroom. Karel and Leroy broke from their kiss to shove down Griff's sweat pants and briefs. Leroy slipped quickly out of his own and pushed Karel's boxers down his legs with impatience. Totally naked again, the three men touched wherever they could. Karel, fulfilling his earlier daydream, ran the fingers of his right hand through the whorls of hair on Griff's chest, pulling at a cluster, then flicking his fingernail over Griff's nipple, hard. Griff groaned deeply, his cock thickening against the top of Karel's thigh. Karel reached back his left hand and interlaced it with Leroy's, tugging the other man closer. He nestled his arse against Leroy's groin, and Leroy rolled his hips so that his cock rubbed up and down the centre crease of Karel's buttocks. Karel's breath caught almost painfully, and he hardened fast, his cock jutting forward against Griff's warm belly.

Griff gave another, more eloquent grunt,

expressing his impatience. *Always impatient!* Karel had rarely had sex where no words were needed, let alone with more than one partner, yet here the action moved seamlessly. Leroy shifted them without fuss so that Griff faced the kitchen counter, and together they bent him forward. Leroy also had condoms to hand within seconds—had they been in that ultra-tidy drawer, too?—passing a rather luridly coloured one to Karel. Leroy helped roll it on, too, jacking Karel's cock lazily but firmly through the latex.

Griff grabbed the edge of the counter until his knuckles turned white, belly cushioning him as Karel thrust in. Behind Karel, Leroy ran his cock between Karel's cheeks, rocking into him as he drove into Griff. When Karel glanced down at the counter, checking that Griff wasn't too uncomfortable, he saw Griff had thrown back a hand and interlaced his fingers with Leroy's.

Karel could have felt like a third wheel, he supposed. Instead, he was oddly thrilled to be between that grasp: to be part of it.

And when the vibration rolled a plate off the counter to smash on the smartly tiled floor, no one was distracted from fucking for a single second.

"Sit with us," Leroy murmured to Karel.

The sex had finished in laughter and swearing and plenty more mess on the floor than that single martyred plate, and after a hurried wipe down of surfaces—both plastic and human—they poured out fresh cups of tea and coffee and ambled to the large, deep sofa in the living room.

In silent co-ordination, they folded themselves down on it, spreading over the three cushions yet still clinging to each other. It took only a moment to find individual positions that kept them both comfortable and close, Karel in the middle. The room was warm enough that none of them brought their discarded clothes from the kitchen, yet cool enough that the new sweat dried slowly, and not unpleasantly, on their skin.

Leroy sighed quietly. "This is what we hoped for, ever since we saw you."

"Hm?"

"Sitting here. All of us. Being together."

"You didn't know me." Karel felt confused, but ridiculously warmed by the comment.

"We wanted to. You're a striking man, Karel. Attractive."

73

He smiled ruefully. "You mean, taller than others in the crowd."

Leroy tutted and ran his hand over Karel's short-cropped head. "I *mean*, more attractive than others."

Karel was embarrassed: there could be no other explanation for his disturbance. "You had no idea what kind of man I was. How I would act, what I cared about. What I would think about you two."

"I kinda knew," Griff said, in his blunt way.

"I kinda *hoped*." Leroy's smile was in everything he did, in every word he spoke.

"I don't know—" Karel began.

"Hush," Leroy said. "Enough talking."

They kissed carelessly, messily, indulgently. A trail of Leroy's saliva trickled down into Karel's beard. He liked that. He liked the way the men made him feel so relaxed physically, both of them, not just the way they got each other off, but before and after too.

"And anyway, we stalked you," Griff murmured on Karel's other side.

"What?"

Leroy tutted at Griff, still smiling. He leaned away from his caressing of Karel for a moment. "That's not what he meant. *Stalking*? Huh. All it was—you'd dropped a voucher out of your pocket when you were at the bar. In the shape of an ice cream. The bartender knew it was for *With A Kick*. The club shares promotions with other local businesses, right?"

Karel nodded, happy to listen to any nonsense if it was in Leroy's slow, sexy voice.

Griff snorted. He'd slipped down on the sofa seat until his head lay almost in Karel's lap. Karel didn't think he could fuck again so soon after the kitchen scene, but Griff's tongue on the crease of his thigh and belly was proving tantalising. "We'd been there a couple of times, before the explosion. So, when Theo—that's the bartender—told us who'd left the voucher, we knew it was a clue to finding you again. So, we started hanging out there, before Leroy's gig each night." Griff's voice was muffled, his breath skimming over Karel's pubic hair. It tickled, but Karel had no intention of asking him to stop. "Watching out for you."

What the hell? Karel wasn't sure how he felt about being pursued like that.

"Hush, Griff," Leroy complained, after a glance at Karel's expression. "You're weirding him out."

"I am?" Griff looked truly horrified. "I just meant we wanted—!"

"It's okay," Karel interrupted gently. Griff seemed to bring that out, a need to console, to reassure. "But I'm not that special."

"Yeah. Right," the dancer on his other side murmured, so low that Karel wasn't sure he heard anything at all.

"And after we made our minds up," Griff said, with a wide yawn that threatened to engulf Karel's stirring balls, "We went for it."

It? Did they mean *him*? Karel was too stunned to respond. Instead, he tugged gently at Griff's ear until Griff slid back up to snuggle beside him. Then he leaned back into the sofa cushion and watched as Leroy leaned over him to kiss Griff, deeply and just as messily as Leroy had kissed Karel before, a delicious home movie less than a foot from Karel's face of two gorgeous men making out. Karel felt he'd been gifted something extraordinarily, sexily intimate.

Griff fell asleep soon after—Karel didn't know how long he'd been awake and already downstairs that morning. Maybe he was a light sleeper anyway. Leroy snuffled a few times, stretching his legs, easing his back, before he started snoring lightly, also dozing. A dancer must have to keep horrifically fit, such athletic routines must take their toll on his body one way or another. Maybe he needed to loosen the kinks after last night's sex. Maybe he took naps all day until his evening session.

Maybe.

Karel brushed his hand over the two heads propped against him. Leroy's dark curls, Griff's shallow fuzz. 'Maybe' was all Karel had of them. So little information, yet so much sensation.

He was a thoughtful man but not an openly emotional one, at least not towards others. His family and friends knew he was compassionate and loyal, but he didn't feel the need to declare himself to everyone he met. At least, not until he had developed a relationship with someone that was likely to continue, at the very least as friendship.

He was as physically sated as he'd ever been, yet his mind wouldn't let him rest. Had Griff been right, during their conversation in the kitchen? Was Karel still single because he couldn't find what he wanted in one man? He had many examples of committed couples in his group of friends, or men who were still happy playing the field.

But perhaps he was somewhere in between.

Was that why, when he'd first come to the area, he'd been drawn to Patrick and Lee? He liked both of them as friends, of course, but he'd also considered them originally as potential lovers. Patrick's steady maturity; Lee's lively youth. Karel would have dated either, very happily. And, if he were honest, and if he didn't have strong respect for their commitment to each other, he would have enjoyed them both together.

He wanted that combination of strength and reliance, excitement and comfort. And if he couldn't find all that he wanted in a single person...

Would he consider joining an established couple?

Chapter 6

Karel hadn't seen Leroy and Griff for a week. He was disappointed—and horribly frustrated. One night of mind-blowing sex, and it was like something had awoken his libido with a particularly loud and insistent trumpet call. He woke every morning with a relentless hard-on and nothing to relieve it except his own hand. He dreamed at night about Leroy's sensuous, supple body; imagined Griff's mouth still on his; smelled the lingering flavour of all three men together, a fascinating mixture of skin, sweat, and that sweet, sumptuous jam Griff had produced for their breakfast. Karel even thought he heard their voices occasionally, in among the jumble of shouts and calls on the site during the day. But whenever he raised his head to check out for certain, it never was.

If it wasn't totally ridiculous, he'd admit to missing them. How could that be? He'd only met them a couple of times, shared an ice cream and a spicy tortilla, and chatted about art.

Oh... and there was that night of mind-blowing sex to add to the equation.

Karel knew the absence was caused by his work. The hotel project was at a critical point, and suddenly one of the hotel managers had decided, yes, they wanted to take part in the arts festival after all. The ongoing work had to be reorganised to make one of the conference rooms available for a local poetry group, and Karel had worked long hours with the other contractors to keep things to the timetable, else they suffered financial penalties. And that would impact everyone's pay packet. Even though everyone was pleased the hotel would be involved in a community event, it wasn't easy to keep the disruption to a minimum in just one part of the building. So, at the end of his day, he had little energy for going out, or calling up friends, or...

Yeah. The mind-blowing sex thing.

Friday evening arrived, when Karel would often go out to join the Soho partying, but he was at home at a loose end instead. Should he enjoy the unexpected extra time to sleep? He had work the next day. Or call his parents? Read the books he'd recently taken out of the Westminster Reference library?

Or he could go back out to Master Mac's for a drink.

He lay on his bed in his small rented room and thought things over. That was his way: he was always honest, always open, but sometimes he needed time to consider carefully the things going on in his life. He needed to make sense of other peoples' reactions. And sometimes his own.

Physically, he was comfy. His rooms were warm enough, and he was lucky with the facilities. The building had been recently painted, inside and out, the furniture was relatively new, and he had access to the laundry room and kitchen whenever he wanted. His landlord never bothered him—except when he needed some DIY help—because he knew Karel was a safe bet as a tenant. The neighbours were okay, mostly young singles, a few professional families, and locals who'd lived here before it became part of the London commuter belt.

So, tonight, he half-dozed, his muscles relaxed after a hot shower, his gaze on a couple of photos of his family pinned on the wardrobe door.

He'd never regretted moving to London, despite missing his family, and he enjoyed the life he'd made for himself. Without boasting, he reckoned—hoped—his friends liked his company, and he had more than enough work to keep him busy through word of mouth recommendations from already satisfied clients.

His work... well. He avoided those thoughts when he could.

He'd never planned a career in the building trade when he moved here, but that was the path he'd taken in the end. *Chosen* to take: he didn't regret many of his decisions. He liked being physically challenged, and he loved creating something useful and necessary. Construction worked well with those parameters. And being self-employed meant he was free to take up any opportunities, spend time with whomever he liked, travel when he wanted, and stay over likewise. He liked blending in, reckoned he was good at it. He was a tall, distinctive man, but he also knew how to listen to others. People fascinated him: it wasn't a chore.

So why the hell did he feel so restless now?

The screen of his laptop flickered in the dimly

lit room: his sister was online. The familiar chime of a Skype call request lasted only a few seconds before she responded. Her hair was twisted up into a tightly-groomed topknot, her wide eyes framed with extravagant lashes. Ada had inherited the beauty gene in his family, he knew.

"Hi, *bratříček*," she said, a little sleepily.

"Sorry, big *ségra*. Did I wake you?" The nicknames—little brother, big sister—were part of their shared history now. And also a family joke, as Ada was still in her twenties and barely over five foot, while Karel was now thirty-five and well over six.

She yawned. "No, it's okay. I've only just got in from work and I guess I'm ready for bed already."

"No fabulous industry dinner and party tonight?" That was the pattern of most of Ada's weekends.

She stuck out her tongue. It made her look twenty years younger, and he laughed. "Nothing wrong with staying in, *miláčik*." She would always be his darling. "I'm home myself."

It was so good to be able to see her rather than just talk by phone. Karel wanted his parents at home to use Skype but he hadn't persuaded them into twentieth century technology yet, let alone twenty-first. It would be so good to see their faces. He hadn't been back to the family home for many months. It took too much money and too much lost work each time. And, to be honest, was often a painful experience. He missed being part of a family, of being with people who knew him so well. But the constant questioning on how his career was going, whether he had a steady partner yet? It was tiring, however well meant.

"So... what's up?" Ada yawned again and glanced at the time on her laptop. "Hey. It's only ten o'clock. Why the hell are you on your own, on a Friday night?"

He shrugged and laughed, but the sound was a little strained.

"I thought you'd made a new set of friends in Soho." She peered suspiciously into the screen as if she could see him closer. "Hey. You know you can't move back in with me, right?" Ada's work was in Canary Wharf and she'd recently moved into a new, much larger apartment in London's Docklands.

"You mean, I'd cramp your style?"

"Too right, *brácha*." Ada snorted happily. She dated a lot, and enthusiastically, with no plans to settle down, much to their parents' distress. "After all, everyone's pretty fluid where I play, and I can't have too many of my dates preferring my bro."

Karel laughed louder. "You're safe. It's been too busy at work for me to have much party time. And my friends have schedules of their own, you know."

"Party time." She snorted again. "Glad you mentioned that, because you need far more of it, Karel. You're too serious, too careful."

"Me?" Karel thought of the warm, oversized bed he'd shared with Leroy and Griff the other night, and couldn't remember ever being less serious.

Ada yawned yet again, leaning back so that her face slipped half out of view of the webcam. "Why don't you come over on Sunday? I've got a couple of friends dropping in for supper. I'd love you to join us. Chybíš mi." *I miss you.*

It sounded a good idea, even though he knew she was probably trying to set him up with one of the guys from her work. Ada was very bright, well-liked, and frighteningly hardworking—the company was already talking about a partnership for her. And she knew everyone there was to know, their tastes, their income, their prospects, and their potential suitability for her more sober, single brother. None of her plans had worked so far, though.

"I'll call you," he said, meaning to accept and keep the timing flexible, but Ada snapped up the hint of hesitation.

"You're seeing someone already. Tell me!"

"No! No, I'm not."

"Is it that cute man with the, what was it, a sweet shop? And his equally cute, younger partner?"

Karel rolled his eyes. "Patrick and I are friends only. It's an ice cream shop. And he and his partner Lee are engaged to be married now."

"Pity," Ada said shamelessly. "Though that doesn't always mean off limits—"

"No," Karel said firmly. He hoped he wasn't blushing. Perhaps a phone call would have been better, after all. "We're all just friends."

Ada nodded. She ran through a few of the things happening at her work, a melodrama where a client promised the same contract to three applicants, a candidate who'd turned up for a prestigious job in the city dressed in cargo shorts and flip flops. Her latest appraisal which was, as usual, excellent.

Karel listened because he loved her, and he liked hearing about her work. He probably would call in to see her on Sunday. He had no work scheduled, no other specific plans, and it would be a good thing to meet her for a decent meal and some easy, familiar conversation...

You're too serious, too careful.

He paused. Because sometimes he reckoned, you *shouldn't* be too careful.

The restless feeling coalesced into a knot of excitement in his belly. He knew exactly why he felt unsettled, and what he was going to do about it. He wanted to go to the club. Tonight. *Now.* A glance at his phone confirmed it was still early in 'Master Mac' hours—the adult floor show wouldn't start for another half hour. Apparently, he wanted to fight for space at the bar, sweat in an over-crowded, too-hot room, listen to loud people having a good time, and drink overpriced beer.

No, not just that. Be honest.

He wanted to meet the two men there, buy Griff a beer, sit beside him, and together they'd watch Leroy dance.

"You'd better go," Ada said with another yawn that almost obscured her wicked grin. "I have no idea what I said that prompted it, *bratříček*, but that predatory look on your face is way too obvious!"

Leroy wasn't dancing when Karel arrived—he

surely hadn't expected that lucky coincidence—and didn't appear for another hour. There was no sign of Griff either. The club was packed tonight, and Karel somehow knew that Griff would struggle with that. He was disappointed not to see him, though. What a difference from their first meeting, when Griff had both startled and insulted him! Karel nursed a beer and leaned more or less comfortably against the bar.

When Leroy was announced, sliding almost shyly onto the small stage, the atmosphere in the room picked up palpably. A group of guys along the bar from Karel raised their beer bottles in cheers and whooped their enthusiasm. Karel was intrigued: he'd been fascinated with Leroy's dancing the very first time he saw it, but it looked like Leroy was a minor celebrity at the club.

The music started low, with a heavy beat, and Leroy swung apparently effortlessly up onto the pole, hitched himself to it with one bent leg, and fell back so his hair brushed the floor. He was wearing shallow, tight-fitting briefs and a sleeveless top in multi-hued satin. In Karel's opinion, Leroy would have looked magnificent in nothing but newspaper, but the glimmer of the fabric as Leroy twisted made Karel's pulse race.

The dance was spectacular, as Griff had once described it. Now that Karel knew the sinews and muscles of Leroy's body from the inside, as it were, the choreography took on a whole new glow. Leroy swung back and forth, at times supported by only one hand or one knee, at other times reaching for the ceiling, then sliding slowly and with astonishing muscle control down to the floor, and finally scooping back up onto his feet with a tilt of his body, like a salute to the audience. It was a tightly rehearsed routine, Karel suspected, but Leroy brought such insouciance and charisma to everything he did that it appeared deceptively easy.

The music swelled to a faster, thicker beat and Leroy reached the top of the pole. A clutch of customers around the stage raised their beer bottles or glasses and yelled encouragement. As Karel watched, his heart in his mouth, Leroy hooked his knee around the pole, tightened his thigh muscles, and spun his way around and down, his back arched and his hands at his side, hurtling towards the ground.

A couple of people cried out in shock or fear, Karel wasn't sure. He found he'd taken a couple of instinctive steps towards the stage. It wasn't as if he'd be able to stop Leroy, but something inside him wanted desperately to catch the man before he harmed himself—

Which, of course, he didn't. Leroy jerked to an impossibly exact halt just before his body would have smashed to the floor. He reached almost languidly to grab the pole and stabilise himself, twisted so that his feet were back on solid ground, and sprang upright to take his applause.

The crowd—as the saying was—went wild. Karel found himself clapping furiously along with everyone else. His heart was beating too fast and his throat was too tight for comfort. Leroy was magnificent, even in the challenging, athletic world of pole dancers. Karel had no idea why he wasn't performing on a more public stage, in front of larger and more discerning crowds.

When Leroy waved to the raucous audience and darted through the curtain at the back, the hubbub in the bar swelled loud again. A group of young, gym-muscled men laughed loudly by Karel's ear. A glass smashed at the back of the bar and someone cursed in an Eastern European dialect that Karel thought he knew. It was like the air had loosened in the club, as if tension had gone and excitement had dulled.

Or was that just how Karel felt? He stayed at the

bar, wondering—he couldn't help it, even if it sounded boastful—if Leroy had spotted him tonight, like before. The next act ambled onto the stage, a young dancer in full camo gear, at least until he started peeling it off. Karel watched him listlessly for a while, but he could see what Leroy had meant when he said the dancer didn't know how to attract the crowd. Several punters moved away from the stage, started chatting to friends, calling for more drinks. This young guy couldn't hold their attention like Leroy had.

And then Griff was there, at the bar. Karel was aware of him even before he pressed against Karel's back and ran his arm around Karel's waist. Griff's grip was a little too fierce for comfort, but when he came face to face, his arms still clinging, Karel didn't move away. The club was in the middle of London, after all, in one of the most cosmopolitan areas: it didn't matter who hugged whom. And somehow he knew Griff wanted—needed—this touch.

"Hi," he said softly, though it was probably difficult to hear over the dance music.

But Griff smiled, his gaze on Karel's mouth. "Hi to you, too."

Griff was in a bright-coloured polo shirt and

faded denim jeans. His thighs looked very good in them, thick, muscled. A few dark chest hairs curled mischievously over the open placket of the shirt.

Karel felt very slightly dizzy. "Did you just arrive?"

Griff pushed his glasses up his nose and nodded, but didn't elaborate. His hands tightened on Karel's hips. "Leroy will be changing out of costume. He'll be on his way any minute now."

Karel was a little amused: it was as if Griff had captured him and didn't want to let go until Leroy joined them. Maybe he was afraid Karel would leave, when that was the furthest thing from Karel's mind. He couldn't even believe he'd stayed away from them for a full week. What the hell had he been thinking? Griff's grip, and the mere promise of Leroy, brought everything flooding back. Karel's whole body seemed to light up, with both fire and illumination.

Leroy sauntered over from a door behind the bar area, obviously where the dancers entered and exited. Both Karel and Griff turned their heads to watch him, as in fact did most of the patrons in the bar. He wasn't wearing much more than when he was on the pole—his jeans were ripped across the knees, his top looked two sizes too small and bared his shoulders to view.

God, he was beautiful. Karel's cock, already plumped up, firmed to a hard shaft. It was near painful, like he hadn't been aroused for a year.

Leroy took no notice of the men watching him, apart from a wave to the bar staff and a fist bump to a couple of people he met on the way over. He came straight to Karel and Griff, greeted Griff with a kiss on the mouth, and then stood on Karel's other side, placing his hand on Karel's chest. He took in a long, exaggerated breath, and briefly closed his eyes in bliss. Karel loved the touch, though he realised the act was making him blush. He didn't do that, though. Did he?

"You haven't called," Leroy said, with the slightest pout. He was still channelling his playful stage persona.

"I checked for messages, too," Griff added. His gaze was darting between the other two, his pupils wide.

Karel resisted reminding them they never gave him their numbers, nor asked for his when he left for work that morning after. But he wasn't going to apologise, either. "I've been busy."

"Oh, and yes, what fucking excuse is that?" Leroy spluttered out. "We're all *busy*, man."

Karel nearly laughed. How ridiculous to see Leroy so outraged, when Karel was just trying to be respectful of everyone's lives. He could have searched them out, he supposed. He could have asked at the club for a contact number. He'd only been to the house once but he had a good memory: he could have found it again, and gone to call on them.

"What's that look for?" Griff, as Karel might have expected, was looking deeper, examining Karel, wrestling out the truth. "You didn't want to call?"

"No, I did. I would have," Karel said calmly. His smile—of pleasure, of happiness—was begging to let loose.

"Did we upset you? Did we disgust you?"

"Griff," Leroy warned.

Karel frowned. "God, no!"

"So why haven't you come to find us?" But Griff had eased off on the angry face and was rubbing his cheek against Karel's. Karel wasn't even sure he realised he was doing it.

"Okay. My fault. I didn't ask for your number—" Leroy began.

"You know where we are," Griff interrupted. "You know Leroy is a regular at the club."

Karel took a deep breath. "I know. But it's true, I

have been busy at work. We don't all have time to play as much as we'd like." He tried not to sound judgemental or resentful, but it was surprisingly difficult.

Griff snorted. "Another excuse. Tell me what the problem is."

"Wait. Let's sit down. Hold that table!" Leroy waved peremptorily at a couple of staff clearing beer bottles and napkins from a nearby booth. Before anyone else could move in there, he prodded the other two over to sit. Karel didn't see him order drinks, but three beers appeared shortly afterwards in front of them.

"So. Your problem?" Griff was like a terrier, but Karel could also see the worry in his eyes.

"It's not a problem. It's... a fact. You're a couple."

"You said that before." Leroy shrugged and took a long draft from his beer bottle. The small beads of condensation ran over his wrist and up his dark, graceful arm. "And yes, we're everything to each other. Or almost, at least. And so..." His gaze was as fierce as Griff's on Karel. "What exactly do you think *you* are?"

Did Leroy mean to be cruel? Karel had never thought himself over-sensitive, but he'd been in emotional turmoil since he met these men, and that *hurt.* "I'm an entertainment, a novelty. I'm a night's fun."

"The morning after, too." Griff grinned.

Karel gave what he suspected was a rather sad smile. "The morning after, too."

Leroy was frowning now. "You didn't enjoy it?"

"Now you *are* being cruel." Karel didn't mean to snap but his disappointment was sharp. "You know I did. I'm not complaining, believe me. It's been great."

"*Been* great? What the fuck does that mean?" Leroy's voice was unusually tight. "How was I cruel? You must know I didn't mean anything like that, man."

"Shut the hell up, the pair of you. You're making everything worse." Griff's voice startled them both. He turned to Karel, face set in a determined expression. "Listen to me. Yeah, I know Leroy speaks for us usually. I'm clumsy with all that. Especially after too many beers."

Karel shook his head. "You say what you mean. That can only ever be the right thing."

Griff grimaced. "Yeah. Maybe. But not always at the right time. I nearly lost you before we'd even got you, with my stupidity at the club that first night we met."

"It's okay—"

"Let me finish, for fuck's sake!" Griff winced as if he'd bitten his tongue. Maybe he had, his words had been so fierce. "I'm just saying, I'm not the man for words. But I know what I want. I know what's good."

Leroy nodded beside him, obviously itching to make amends. "What's good is, we got a second chance to meet you. To seduce you. Right?"

Karel nodded. He had been seduced, well and truly. It would take him a long while to forget the perfection and passion of that.

Leroy's hand on his neck surprised him, the fingertips familiar yet freshly exciting, still soft with the grip powder he used. Leroy turned Karel's head, pushing him towards... Griff's kiss, the man's lips slick and soft, his breath short and almost pained as he reached for Karel.

Karel had no time to think about who was around, who may see them. *Who cares?* He kissed back, furious with his eagerness, loving it equally. Leroy sat close to his side, his breath on the junction of Karel's collarbone, his fingers teasing up under Karel's shirt, pressing him into Griff's kisses, his touches hidden from view, yet branding Karel with every stroke.

"We want you," Leroy said, his voice husky.

"Now," Griff added, breathlessly. "Again."

Karel smiled and sighed, whether from resignation or delight, he wasn't totally sure. But his heart sang either way, because he knew his acquiescence had never been in doubt.

Chapter 7

Karel thought he could sleep in that huge bed for ever: nestle there with two warm, deep-breathing bodies that were so different individually, yet so consuming in partnership.

This time, he woke in the morning with just Griff. The man lay sprawled on the mattress beside him, arms flung wide. For a long moment, Karel lay still, just breathing in the rich smell of male skin. It mixed intriguingly with the lingering tang of lemon soap from the next-door bathroom, and the faint aroma of cut grass from outside the building. Leroy must have opened the bedroom window when he woke to take a shower. Karel thought he could hear Leroy whistling in another room, though he couldn't have said which one. The flat was ridiculously large, and not just compared to his own place.

Griff made a grumbling noise beside him and turned his head towards Karel. He was awake, quite suddenly, unlike Leroy's slow return to consciousness the previous time Karel had stayed the night. Griff flapped his hand around on the bedside table until he found his glasses and put them on.

"Good morning." Karel reached over a hand and cupped Griff's face.

"You wanna stay over?" Griff said abruptly. Behind the lenses his eyes shone with lazy pleasure.

"Here, at your flat? Tempting, but no, thank you, I have to work today. Saturday's often a working day for me, the same as any other. And the hotel where I'm based? The schedule's changed up, so they can host some of the festival events."

"Which is good..."

"Yes. But it's extra, unexpected work for me."

"After that, though."

"What do you mean? I can come over tonight. I'd love to—"

"Not just that." Griff flushed deeply. "I mean to move in. To live with us."

Karel's heartbeat sped up, but he wisely decided

not to laugh, or scorn such a startling idea. He was becoming used to Griff's bluntness. "That's a big decision to take so quickly, don't you think?"

"No. I don't." But Griff's nose crinkled as he frowned, sending the glasses back down to the tip of his nose. "We're good together."

"That's sex," Karel said gently, though his throat felt tight. "That's not the same as being together all the time." Jesus, he hoped he wasn't patronising Griff again. But the guy seemed to have such a simplistic, naïve expectation of life.

"Is it the condoms?" Griff blurted.

"The...?"

"Condoms. So many of 'em. And we don't always take time to find the best fit. I mean, you're a big guy."

I mean, am I really? Karel was amused by being described so frankly by his penis size—and at the implied compliment—so this time, he did laugh, though gently. "I don't mind at all. I'm used to them. They can be fun."

"Some guys don't agree. But Leroy buys them all the time, always trying new shit. I hate the peppermint ones, though." Griff's nose crinkled again. "We don't always use them when it's just us, we're tested regularly. So, we can stop them anytime. When we find someone to do it for, of course. You know what? We should all get checked out together. Today, tomorrow. Soon." His voice gentled. "I'd love to feel you without a cover."

Oh God. Karel's skin lit up as if he'd been doused in chilled, sparkling water. "Griff, it's not that. I'm just... used to being on my own, I suppose. Looking after myself."

"I'd look after you." Griff's voice was quiet, strangely ragged. "I'd want to."

Astonishingly moved, Karel was stunned into silence. His hand stilled on Griff's face, where he'd been gently stroking a stray, twisted tuft of his beard. "Thanks."

"Hm." Griff shook himself, like a dog that's been in the rain, needing to shed the dampness, careless of whoever else was in range. It seemed to clear his mood. "You looking for something more, then?"

"Yes. I... yes, I think I am."

Griff nodded, then was quiet for what seemed like a long time. Until he shifted in the bed, placing a hand firmly on Karel's belly, and said, "You wanna have sex now?"

It seemed that was his strategy for every awkward moment, yet Karel felt a burst of desire in his belly that ached not just for the physical release, but sex with Griff. "Come here," he murmured, and opened his arms.

The kissing, as always, was enthusiastic and intense. Griff was wearing nothing but his glasses, which soon rolled off his face and onto the floor. Karel had pulled his boxers back on during the night, but without breaking the kiss, they quickly yanked them off. Now both naked, Karel slid his hand back down Griff's belly to find Griff's erection, thick and very hard. He tightened his palm around their cocks together, letting the pre-cum dribble between them to ease the stroking. Griff spat into his hand and added more lubrication to them both, then rested his hand on top of Karel's. As Karel slowly but firmly jacked them off, Griff's tongue slipped out to lick his lips—Karel's, too.

A sliver of morning light through the bedroom window shook in and out of focus on their joined hands. The sound of distant traffic was almost drowned out by Griff's loud, desperate panting. Their sweat and the sweet aroma of impending seed overlay the garden smells.

The ache in Karel's groin was poignant, hot, and very, very good.

A sudden "Oh!" was all Griff said, but in such a

strangled tone that Karel knew he was coming soon. His palm felt dangerously wet and he was afraid he'd lose his grip on them both. Then his balls tightened, he started to come first, and grip was the last thing he was thinking about.

As Griff clutched him tightly through his climax, Karel caught a movement out of the corner of his eye. At some point, Leroy had come to stand in the bedroom doorway. He was dressed in a loose T-shirt and sweatpants, his hair damp from washing and clipped away from his neck and forehead. He leaned on one shoulder against the door frame, his arms folded casually over his chest. He was smiling contentedly.

How much had he heard of the conversation with Griff, when Griff asked Karel to move in? Karel didn't know. Leroy's relaxed pose implied not only was he okay with Karel screwing Griff, he welcomed it. As Leroy watched them, the colour heightened on his cheeks and his chest moved faster than before, his breath getting shorter. There was no mistaking the thicker bulge in his groin: he deliberately slid his hand inside the front of his sweats and jerked a couple of times at his cock. He met Karel's gaze, his eyes wide, his expression urging Karel on.

"Karel!" Griff whispered his name, groaned, and came in turn all over Karel's fisted hand. Karel ran his free hand down to Griff's arse, pulling him closer so that the spilled cum slicked their bellies. The brush of Griff's beard against his morning stubble was rough and thrilling, Griff's morning breath rich but uniquely his. Karel didn't really have time or care to spend on anyone but the man in his arms. However, he could spare one mischievous second to glance back at Leroy. And wink. Then return to post-sex relaxation with Griff.

Nonetheless, he was secretly satisfied to hear Leroy groan behind them both, as he came abruptly and uncontrollably in his sweats.

Karel wasn't prepared to move in with them, but over the coming weeks he started to spend much more time at their flat. His place seemed a broom closet in comparison, whereas at Griff and Leroy's flat, he had a wonderful, well-appointed place to stretch out in. He was a large man, and not only in body size: he liked to have space around him to think and move comfortably. They let him leave his stuff in a spare room when he came around, and there was a generous bathroom with both bath and shower. It was a previously unknown joy to soak in a hot bath after a hard day on site.

The kitchen continued to be the one place they met, ate and chatted together at the beginning and end of each day. And Karel spent most nights in bed with the other two. They didn't always have sex—though, who was he kidding? They almost always did, in one form or another—but he grew to love the relaxed, generous loving they gave to him. It was the same as they gave to each other, and although he worried at first that he'd be disturbing their familiar routine, they barely broke step to include him in the household. He picked up his share of the chores, contributed to meals and drinks, and even persuaded them into watching more TV sport, though the trade-off—which didn't worry him too much *at all*—was to share some of their more edgy porn downloads.

He also learned that, during the day, Leroy was often out at a local community youth centre where he ran voluntary exercise and dance classes, and Griff hosted a busy cookery blog from a rather frighteningly high-tech PC in a corner of the living room. Karel felt there was something new to discover about the men he was dating, every day.

The guys worked apart and together, but they were always an emotional unit—and now they were three.

No one seemed to worry if Karel wasn't at his best, if he was too shattered after work to talk, if he was angry at the behaviour of some of the contractors at the site, if he needed some quiet time to chat to Ada and his family. In return, he coped when Griff was in one of his bleak, argumentative moods, or Leroy was grumpy with back pain, or too hyped up from dancing to pay attention to any boring domestic plans. Karel could work the hours he needed, then come back to good company, great sex, and a comfortable home.

Home. It was a word he was growing to love, rather than a mere description. He'd never realised how *much* he missed company, until this new arrangement—this new kind of family. It was something increasingly precious to him. He and the other two men laughed a lot together, at the best and the most ridiculous moments. And it was because they were happy.

Another exciting discovery—other than the amazing fact of him living and sleeping with two men with almost total ease—was the studio. Leroy had showed it to him after he'd been visiting for a couple of weeks. And now, whenever Leroy needed to rehearse a new routine for the club, Karel would find an excuse to join him for a while.

It had blown him away from the start.

The flat stretched the depth of the building, with more space at the back than appeared from the front door. A third of that floor space had been converted into a single dance studio, with tall windows reaching almost from floor to ceiling, overlooking the small back yard, and fitted out with plain cloth blinds, warm wooden flooring—and nothing else. Karel had never been in such an unencumbered, yet atmospheric space. Leroy, or his mother, had placed a free-standing dance barre in front of a full-size mirror that covered almost half of one wall, and there was a practice pole in the corner.

However, it was the other side of the room that had immediately caught Karel's attention, with a delight that snatched the breath from his body. That was where the sunlight burst through, sweeping an arc across the plain wood and dappling shadows on the window frames. Clear of furnishing, it was a bubble of perfection, several yards square. It made an artistic statement in itself, let alone offering a setting for anything more.

It would be a magnificent space for an artist to work. He couldn't help the thought.

On a quiet Tuesday morning, when his shift didn't start until after lunch, and Griff was hammering away on his keyboard in some programming language or other, Leroy had drawn him along the corridor and into the studio.

"You like this place, don't you?" Leroy nudged against him, twisting in casual yet fluid steps, as if drawing Karel into a dance.

"You know I do! It's magnificent."

"Yes, there is a certain twist of awe on your handsome face," Leroy teased. "You're a dancer? I never asked…"

"No." Karel felt his throat tighten.

"Tell me." Leroy stopped wriggling and stood in front of him. He put one palm to Karel's chest, a familiar gesture of his, but even though it was just a touch, it still felt as if he'd given Karel a full body hug. "The look on your face, every time we come in here… you're glowing."

Karel laughed self-consciously yet, just perhaps, it was a rare time when he wanted to talk about it. "I… do some art, at least I used to, when I had time and the space. This would be a superb art studio, as well as a practice area. Of course, you must need it all for your dancing."

"Just the area around the barre. Not much else."
Leroy shrugged, his gaze still fixed on Karel's face.
"It could easily be both."

"No! I didn't mean... I wasn't asking." Karel was
horrified that, for a blissful, selfish moment, he'd
even considered the possibility. "I need so much
space. I'd make such a mess. It'd be... no, it wouldn't
be right. It's your place. You're the artist."

"There's no single art, no single artist, man."

Karel gave a snort. "You are so pretentious
sometimes."

"I am, right? Goes with the territory." Leroy
laughed, never insulted. "But seriously, why not, if
I'm happy with that?"

Distract him. It was a familiar, and effective
strategy, and Karel used it when he needed to. "Is
this flat yours, Leroy? I mean..."

"Hey. It's okay to ask, how do a pole dancer and
an unemployed chef afford a place like this? It's my
mother's, an inheritance from her godparents' will.
They were friends of her parents, and enthusiastic
art patrons—they supported Mum's dancing career
when she was growing up, but wanted her to have
assets of her own, for when that career was over.
She owns the flat outright, and there was enough

money left in the will for an annuity that pays the property taxes. So, she knows she always has a base for when she's in London."

"She travels a lot with her ballet troupe?"

"Yeah. To be honest, the last time she was back in the UK was almost a year ago, and at the moment she's away all the time. She's always been nervous of the flat being left empty in between visits, so we agreed a few years ago that I—we—would live here and look after the place. We just have to pay for food and the utilities, and she gets free caretakers, right?" His eyes softened for a moment as he looked around the room. "She also knows how much I appreciate this studio."

"She knows you're dancing?"

Leroy smiled with spontaneous, genuine pleasure. "I've always been dancing! Neither Mum, Dad, or teachers could ever stop me. They only pushed me into gymnastics in the hope it would soak up some of my excess energy. Which it did—but I returned to dancing in the end."

"And the pole dancing?"

"Yeah. Well." Leroy frowned. "She'd prefer it if I were in ballet or theatre."

Karel felt a strong protectiveness on Leroy's behalf. "I didn't mean that in a dismissive way.

Your set is superb. It has strong elements of both."

Leroy gazed at him for a long moment, pleasure twinkling in his eyes. Then he nodded and twisted away to the barre. "Stay here with me for a while, will you? I like you to watch me."

"Of course. I like watching you, too."

Karel hunkered down in a corner of the room where Leroy kept a supply of bottled water, and towels. The wooden floor was warm and comfy under his socked feet. He gestured to the iPod in its dock, and Leroy waved airily for him to select some music. It didn't seem to matter what Karel chose.

Leroy did some warming up exercises, stretching his limbs in a way that seemed amazing and physically scary to Karel, who was muscular in a whole different way. Dressed in his familiar vest and thin sweat pants, Leroy balanced one foot up on the barre, dipped his head to his knee, then turned to repeat on the other side. Then he started moving his feet through a routine that was precise and graceful. Karel had never seen formal dance moves—he'd never watched any ballet at all—but he imagined Leroy was running through the traditional positions that Ada had once talked about. As a child, she'd taken dance exams for a time.

And then the music switched to a techno beat, and Leroy launched into something far livelier.

The new sequence was so different from the pole dancing that Karel was struck with a new awe. Leroy's grace and elegance still shone through, as did his athletic strength. He bent and stretched as he did on the pole, hands on the floor, then reaching for the ceiling, one leg poised behind him, lifted almost to the hip, then hugged up to his belly in front, his back curled over his knee like a beautiful, spineless, human hedgehog. But here, and now, he utilised the floor as he couldn't in the club. Firstly, feet landing on the wood with a strong slap of his soles, and a scuttling, delicate, backwards shuffle, then a magnificent run and leap, again and again, in circles around the floor. He paused abruptly yet with perfect timing, his head steadily facing the mirror, his torso and legs twisting as he spun on the spot.

It was an exhilarating few minutes before Karel realised there was no longer any background soundtrack: the iPod had run into a momentary silence. But the movements were musical in themselves. The control Leroy had over his limbs was awesome, not that Karel hadn't realised that, every time he saw Leroy cling to the pole by the back of his knee alone, or swing upside down with just one hand and his other, inner arm.

Leroy stopped again, rather breathless, and relaxed with his head down and his hands on his thighs. The back and underarms of his vest were dark with sweat. When the iPod decided to wake up and began playing a slower jazz track, he glanced up and grinned at Karel. Small beads of sweat glinted on his face and shoulders. "Dance with me."

Karel burst out laughing.

"No, I mean it." Leroy sauntered over to Karel, in a way that he surely knew was sexy as hell. He slid his arms around Karel's neck and started to sway against him.

Karel felt like a lump of concrete compared to Leroy's sinuous body, and said so.

Leroy snorted. "Just move with the beat. I know you have rhythm, I've heard you singing in the shower."

"What the—?"

"Get over yourself! The bathroom's heard worse, like when Griff's in there. He can't hold a tune in a bucket." Leroy's hands slid down to Karel's hips. "Come on. Just slide your feet. *Mm.* You feel good."

Karel didn't agree. Well, actually he *did* feel

good, but that was because he was holding Leroy close, and the man's body was damp and hot, the skin still shivering from the effort of that magnificent display. But he let Leroy lead him round in a gentle, circular path. Leroy leaned his head on Karel's shoulder and tightened his hands on Karel's hips as they shuffled around, until Karel's feet moved more easily and surprisingly smoothly on the floor, and he realised he was actually swaying in time with the music, and with small— extremely small—but definite style.

"Don't you dance when you go clubbing?" Leroy murmured in his ear. His eyes were half-closed, from what Karel could see, as if he were lulling himself into sleep. "I can feel your strength in every step, and you move beautifully for a large man. Well, we know that already, don't we? At least, my arse does."

Karel chuckled. He was enjoying this, despite himself. "This is a dance studio, Leroy, not a bed. And no, I don't usually dance. If I talk to anyone, it's at the bar, or at a table. I like to watch dancers, whether they're professional like you, or just enjoying themselves. But my sister is the dancer in the family."

"Is that... Ada, that's her name?"

Karel nodded. The lilting movements were relaxing him too. "She's a great dancer, just for her own pleasure, that is. She wishes she had time to take more lessons, as she did in school days. She'd like to dance better."

"We all wish to get better," Leroy said, so softly Karel barely caught it. The iPod ran to another natural stop, and so did the dancing. They opened bottles of water and sat back down on the floor, relaxing side by side.

Karel ran an aimless finger along Leroy's muscular thigh where it pressed against his own. "It must be wonderful to dance as you do. You look transformed by it."

"You think you don't? It's not about following the rules, man. It's about letting go. We'll do it again, I insist. I can't remember ever seeing you smile quite like that."

Karel reckoned Leroy was right. He laughed plenty, especially now he was with them. But there'd been a particular joy in just moving around the room in another man's arms. In Leroy's arms. And then, as he took another, casual draft of his water, Leroy caught him unawares.

"So what kind of artist are you?"

Leave it, Karel wanted to say but, for once, the

joy of sharing his art was stronger than the pain of ignoring it. "Sculpture."

"How fabulous." Leroy wasn't teasing or scorning. He looked genuinely amazed. "You must tell Griff, he would love to see your work. You should—"

"No," Karel interrupted, calmly but firmly. "Those days... are gone for the present. It's not important in my life right now. What is important, is to have a good job, make a secure life."

Leroy peered at him for a long moment. When he spoke, it was as if he were choosing his words very carefully, and still not sure if he'd made the right choice. "Is that really the most important thing for you, Karel?"

Karel's heart tightened briefly as if an open space inside him had just closed in on itself. "Security is one of the most critical needs, isn't it? Somewhere to live, food to eat, to be able to look after your loved ones. That's what matters before anything else. I don't really want to talk about it, Leroy. It's not you." He smiled a little sadly at the cliché. "It's me."

The absence hurt. He was always surprised at how much, even after a couple of years. He'd intended to sign on at a college in the UK when he moved here, to study art. Maybe to make a career of it. He'd been praised at home in the Czech Republic, but no one was ever going to see his work over there. Whereas *London*...

They had been big but, ultimately, unattainable dreams. First priority was to pay some bills, right? No one ever said art guaranteed money. So, he got a job with regular pay and plenty of hours. Maybe it was only going to be for a while, but gradually, it took up all his time, and exhaustion wasn't exactly conducive to artistic inspiration. London rents were crippling, too, even for his tiny flat. Then his mother was ill a year back, and he needed to send her money to help out. Ada helped where she could, but at that time, she was still working her way up the corporate ladder at her firm. No, he'd realised early on he couldn't afford the money to rent studio space, let alone buy decent materials. And when he'd taken on the work at *With A Kick*, even though it wasn't arduous, he'd realised how much he already had going on in his life. It had always been his plan to take a couple of years out from art, build up his savings, then reconsider things another time.

That *another time* just hadn't happened.

"Karel? Don't be sad, man." Leroy slipped a hand

under Karel's T-shirt, his fingers stroking the skin of Karel's belly. It was a strangely poignant caress.

"I'm fine. Don't worry about me. I'm happy with what I have."

"You mean, security? Food and a bed?"

"And looking after loved ones," Karel teased him gently. *Distracting again.* "You are important to me, too. You and Griff."

"Loved ones." Leroy didn't make it a question. "That's how we feel about you, too. I just wish you could relax more with that."

"I'm perfectly relaxed." Some sliver of defensiveness made him snap out, "We can't all lead as careless a life as you do."

A pained expression darted across Leroy's face, gone so fast Karel thought he'd imagined it.

"Careless, eh?"

Shit. The mood in the room was suddenly more tense. "I didn't mean—"

"Hush. No problem." Leroy smiled, rose to his knees and leaned over Karel to kiss him. "Is this careless?"

"What...?" But his pulse began racing at the glint in Leroy's eyes.

Leroy shed his sweats and underwear like Karel had once seen a snake lose its skin on a TV programme—with a wiggle and a shifting of his hips, his movements graceful, fascinating, determined. His vest followed them onto the pile on the floor, then he pushed Karel firmly to lie back on the floor. The wood was smooth yet surprisingly flexible: his builder's brain wondered what materials the fitters had used when they furnished the studio.

"Am I showing enough care now?" Leroy murmured. His erection bobbed eagerly on his thigh, its tip glistening. He got aroused more quickly than anyone Karel had ever known. Now he ran his hand along it mischievously, the laughter back in his eyes, and excitement in his voice. "Why don't you show me how it's done?"

Karel reached for him, clumsy with desire, so desperate to touch the naked man, to welcome his stroking hands and feel his bare, clinging legs around him. "You're so beautiful," he blurted out.

"Says you, the handsome one," Leroy scoffed. He peeled Karel's T-shirt over his head, flipped his jeans open with practised ease, and lifted his hot, aching cock out into the cooling air of the room. "The one with the muscles to keep me pinned down, if he chose. Who could trap me under him. Who could bend me over that barre with a single, strong hand, open up my arse in full view of the mirror, and just—"

The end of Leroy's sentence was lost as Karel sprang to his feet, pulling Leroy with him. He spun Leroy to face the wall and pressed him up against the barre.

"Jesus." Leroy gasped, his hands gripping the ash pole, his gaze fixed on their joint reflection. "You're really gonna do it."

Karel didn't grace that with a reply. The barre was far enough away from the mirror that he could bend Leroy right over, with Leroy slightly up on his toes. Karel had no worries that Leroy could hold that pose for as long as necessary. He ran his hands over the smooth buttocks; ran his fingers down between them, prising them apart. The skin was sweaty there, Leroy's entrance puckered and dark with promise.

Leroy groaned and his head dropped down towards his chest.

Karel took a moment to kick off his jeans, briefs, and socks, then took a long, proper look at their reflection. *How hot is that?* He stood facing the mirror, completely nude, his broad torso in view over Leroy's stooped body. His legs were stockier than Leroy's, the skin paler, the hair thicker. He leaned forward and placed his hands on the pole, either side of Leroy's, bracketing him. Their biceps strained together: Leroy's unruly curls brushed the underside of Karel's chin.

Then Leroy lifted his head enough that his eyes were visible in the mirror. The light in them was jewel-bright, wicked with need. He deliberately lifted his left leg and perched his knee on the barre. It raised his hips another couple of inches and spread his thighs wide open. His arse nudged back into the harbour of Karel's groin.

They'd given up using condoms just a week ago—Griff had, indeed, persuaded them all to get checked out together, soon after they first met, and the test period had passed surprisingly quickly. Maybe because they continued to make condoms a part of their games, and Karel had never felt frustrated by them. But now? He'd never been so pleased he could go without. He spat generously on one hand and slid a finger into Leroy, testing his access, lubricating his way. Leroy wriggled impatiently, ready for him. Karel slid in with care— he wasn't entirely sure what strain the barre would take, to be honest—and they both moaned with delight. The wood creaked beneath them as he pumped slowly and deeply, in and out of Leroy.

Leroy wasn't always bothered about anal sex, enjoying all the other ways of getting off, but today this was a primal pleasure they both enjoyed. Karel watched the reflection as he and Leroy jerked back and forth over the barre, their skin glistening with new sweat, their muscles tightening and loosing, their hips rocking together. Leroy released one hand to reach down for his cock, to stroke himself, though it was an awkward angle with his leg bent up on the pole.

He'll manage.

Just as Karel felt his balls clench, ready to come, the iPod burst back into life with a Kylie mega dance mix. He couldn't have held back if his life depended on it, and the sudden, gleeful pop beat matched his rhythm ridiculously well, but it was a weird feeling to start a climax on a global number one album hit. He laughed as he came, just as Leroy so often did. Leroy hiccupped beneath him, his own laughter strangled with a cry of completion as he came as well, dripping onto the floor.

Their gazes met in the mirror, Karel's vision clouded with bliss, Leroy's face flushed with a self-satisfied grin.

Can't get you outta my head, Karel thought, and it was like an epiphany.

Chapter 8

A couple of weeks later, Karel found himself back at *With A Kick*. He was a much more regular customer nowadays—he and Leroy would visit the shop a couple of afternoons a week, if Karel had finished work and Leroy had time before his set. Sometimes Griff would join them, though only if he'd been able to travel from Regents Park with Leroy. He wasn't happy to travel on the Tube on his own. Karel could appreciate that: there were days it felt more like a cattle truck than transport for London's public.

Today Karel was on his own, though, having finished early on site when the electrical installation took scheduled priority. Although he was looking forward to getting back to the flat, he'd decided to stop in at *With A Kick* on the way, to buy some ice cream for them all to have after supper. He'd done this before, and Patrick let him use an insulated bag to keep it frozen during his Tube journey.

"The usual?" Patrick asked conversationally, as Karel's turn came at the counter, and Karel nodded his thanks: he and his men liked a selection of flavours. He'd been waiting behind a bunch of young people carrying clipboards with pages from the *A-Z* on them, and fashionable messenger bags slung over their shoulders, giggling at the provocative ice cream names, and anguishing over which ones to choose to eat today. One of them snapped a couple of shots of the inside décor of *With A Kick*, before they all shuffled over to a couple of tables.

"Are they to do with the arts festival?" Karel asked. There was still a couple of months before the events started. "Or do all your customers take souvenir shots of the shop?"

They were alone at the counter now, and Patrick laughed freely. "You'd be surprised how many tourists do take photos. I think we've gained quite a reputation on the indie traveller circuit. I have Phiz and his marketing efforts to thank for that. Though on days when kids are snapping their phones right in my face, I'm not so sure it's a blessing."

Karel, in no particular hurry for his takeaway, stood to one side in case more customers came in, but business had calmed for a while.

"It'll get busy again this evening, when businesses finish for the day, and out-of-towners arrive for the theatres," Patrick explained. He huffed a little as he scooped down into the bottom of one particular carton.

Karel smiled to himself: it always took Patrick longer to serve up the ice cream than it did Lee. Patrick was the maestro designer of the flavours, but Lee had the customer work down to a fine art.

"So, how are things with you?" Patrick asked.

"They're good. Very good." Karel couldn't keep the smile off his face these days. Long, relaxing, anticipatory days and nights with Griff and Leroy had brought something very astonishing into his life. It continued to amaze him how his world had been turned around from the day he met them. And yet, if asked, he couldn't say they did anything miraculous or extraordinary with their time together.

On the evenings Leroy wasn't dancing at the club, he'd practise for a couple of hours in the studio, and Karel and Griff would either watch a movie, or play increasingly frenetic games of cards. Griff was frighteningly sharp—to the extent Karel suspected he counted the damned cards—and so Karel kept it to games of fun rather than gambling in any way. Griff was still determined to win, and it was a struggle to Karel's pride to lose anything, even a fun game of cards, so there were often voices raised in protest by the end of it.

Or they might spend time searching through new cookbooks. Bookshop parcels arrived very regularly for Griff, though Karel couldn't help noticing they were for Leroy's account. Karel didn't profess to be any good at cooking, and however much it irritated Griff—who maintained on his rather confrontational blog that any bloody idiot could cook if they just followed a recipe with decent attention—Karel's attempts to follow the recipes usually ended in a charred signature on the base of any pan. But he liked to act as Griff's sous chef, collecting and chopping the vegetables, listening to Griff's commentary on what went well with what, what would curdle or clash in flavour, what new experiments he wanted to try and what ingredients were needed when they next did the online grocery shop. Even without Griff trialling new recipes on his blog, it was a full-time job, cooking something to suit them all. Karel needed fuel, Griff constantly needed novelty, and Leroy just needed to be reminded to eat.

Some evenings, Karel joined Leroy in that fabulous studio for his own workout. His job was physically taxing, but when he'd spent more time on planning than actual construction, he liked to let off steam otherwise. He was still wary of the room's cool, clean beauty—or was it more envy than nervousness that he felt there?—but he enjoyed some light weight training. And, of course, the occasional dance with a sweaty, sensual Leroy. It didn't always end in sex, but sometimes... sometimes it did.

The sex between the three of them never got boring. It wasn't a routine, and the initial desperation for each other had calmed a little. They didn't scale and smother and seduce each other's bodies every night. But the joy of possibility was always there. They slept together, without fail, even the time when Griff had a stinking cold, or when Leroy had brief food poisoning—from a takeaway meal, a mistake Griff wouldn't let him forget—or when Karel came around one night heavily bruised from a doorframe that had accidentally fallen on him on site. In bed, their bodies slipped into the familiar routine, Leroy curled up like a hedgehog, Griff splayed out like a human sacrifice, and Karel...

Between them. Or sometimes beside them. But always right there with them.

"What's that smirk for?" Curtis had appeared unexpectedly at his shoulder, leaning on the counter. Karel had bonded with the canny young delivery man who'd encouraged him to help with restoring *With A Kick* after the explosion. Curtis was sharp, plain-speaking, and self-sufficient, characteristics which appealed to Karel. They'd both worked in and for hotels over the years, and Curtis told a very entertaining story about how he first met his boyfriend Riley in the delivery bay of a posh hotel, where Riley had knocked flat a homophobic chef.

"Needed ice on those knuckles for days," Curtis had scoffed, though his eyes shone at Riley's bravado on his behalf.

Now, he joined Karel while they waited for Patrick to finish scooping Karel's selection of ice cream into a plastic container. Griff loved the biscuit wafers to go with it, but Karel had brought home a whole packet of them recently, so he knew Griff was set up with supplies.

Home. The instinctive pleasure still caught him by surprise.

"Remember those materials you wanted me to look out for?" Curtis said.

Karel couldn't recall for a moment... then he did, and the memory twisted something inside his gut. A few months ago, he'd asked Curtis to look out for certain upholstery materials, not because he was building his own sofa, as Curtis first teased, but because he'd wanted to start a new sculpture. He'd had a sudden inspiration for a small but bold piece, which would look wonderful in the *With A Kick* shop. Karel had never been possessive with his art—he liked to share it with friends and customers—and it had seemed a great way to pay back Patrick and Lee for their friendship. Assuming they liked it, of course.

But as he recalled, the base he'd started on was shoved into a corner in his Wandsworth room, collecting dust. It wasn't material he was short of, it was space and time.

"Are you still interested?" Curtis asked, unaware of Karel's dilemma. "There's a major re-fit happening at an old cinema in Shoreditch. I'm delivering around that area, and they've offered me first pick of the old fittings, as long as I take it all away. There's some amazing stuff there. Unusual fabrics, bizarre little decorations. Great potential for an artist like you, I'd think."

Patrick looked up with a surprised smile. "You're starting your art work again?"

Dammit. "Thanks," Karel said to Curtis, frowning, "but I'll have to pass at the moment. I just don't have the time."

There was a moment's pause and he wondered if he'd somehow got the tone of his voice wrong. Patrick was concentrating again, a little too carefully, on the ice cream scoop, and Curtis raised his eyebrows in a totally obvious way.

"Well, that's fine," Curtis said, but the eyebrows said something different. "Any time you need materials, just let me know."

"Have you got time to sit and have a coffee?" Patrick said quietly to Karel. "I can keep your ice cream in the freezer until you go."

Karel may not have been in a rush, but he didn't have time to be quizzed by Patrick about his artistic aspirations, however well meant. "Thanks, but I'll catch you later. How much do I owe for the takeaway?"

He handed over the money and, as Patrick turned to the till, Lee came bouncing out of the back room where the shop ran its finance and administration work. In one hand he had a batch of print-outs, in the other a deep glass dish of ice cream.

"Patrick has a surprise for you!" he announced to Karel.

"For me?" Karel said, surprised.

"I do?" Rather more worryingly, Patrick also sounded startled.

"Patrick likes creating signature dishes for his friends. And you three come in so often, we thought you deserved a special ice to share." Lee delivered the glass of ice cream with the finesse of a prestigious chef.

Karel stared at it. "Three scoops. Different colours."

"Yes. They're each infused with flavoured gins. Patrick's clever like that, right? Leroy said he likes gin, and so I assumed you probably all did."

"Yes. We... do."

Patrick was tapping something into the till display, but Karel noticed him suddenly stiffen.

"Here's the strawberry with rhubarb and ginger gin." Lee chattered on. "Then pistachio with wild berry gin. And on top of it all, the chocolate ice. Can you believe it? There's a chocolate gin to go with it. And overall, with the triple scoop theme, Phiz suggested we call it—"

"Lee?" Patrick whirled around, his eyes wide with alarm. "Wait! We haven't agreed anything of the sor—"

"—Top and Tails!" Lee announced gleefully.

There was a shocked, sudden, too long silence at the counter.

Lee blinked hard a few times but chattered on obliviously. "Well, I was keen on a pun on construction work, but while we were looking at some DIY online sites, Phiz got dovetail joints mixed up in his head with the way you top and tail the berries for infusion in the gin. Then somehow, it got to be one top and two tails..." He glanced between the other three men. Patrick looked horrified, Curtis was trying desperately not to laugh—his face was scarlet, his hand clamped over his mouth—and Karel suspected his own expression was somewhere north of stunned.

"Bugger," Lee said again, but a little more weakly. "I suppose that could be... taken... the wrong way. Right?"

Curtis took his hand away and roared with laughter.

"It was a joke," Patrick said slowly. The muscles

of his face were very tense and his gaze skittered away from Karel's. "A private joke between those guys. We still haven't named it anything specific." He was trying not to glare at Lee, that was obvious: his eyes were dark and his jaw set, but he wouldn't turn his head Lee's way. "We understand we need a name that's fun and attention-grabbing without being too... personal. Or offensive in any way. We, or our products, would not, at any time, presume to make comment on yours—or anyone's—sex life."

"Sounds like the terms and conditions on one of those medical adverts," Curtis said gleefully.

And then Karel laughed. How could he not? He'd spent several glorious nights this week with his two men, topping the both of them to his heart's content, and to their mutual delight, desire, and mess on the sheets—and now there was going to be an ice cream named for them. And very aptly, it seemed.

"I am honoured," he said. "No, seriously," he added when Curtis spluttered another laugh. "But I think I will take that offer of coffee. To... well. Maybe to calm my nerves."

Patrick had finished apologising. Lee had slunk back into the kitchen in partial disgrace—though it sounded like he was chuckling as he went—and Karel had accepted the offer of free coffee for at least a century, as compensation.

"It's okay," he said, for what felt like the hundredth time. "It's actually very amusing as a double entendre."

"Or a treble," Patrick said glumly. He was on his second consolation coffee in the same time it had taken Karel to drink one. "But whatever the... er... sleeping arrangements, you do seem to have found something special there."

"Yes. Yes, I have."

"Have you moved in to their place yet?"

"I will. Soon." He'd been thinking he would surrender his flat when the lease came up in a couple of months' time. His landlord had already said he'd be happy to extend the tenancy, but Karel had asked for time to think about it. Leroy and Griff welcomed him enthusiastically every time he stayed and never asked for his whereabouts at other times, but he could also see their disappointment if he didn't go to theirs of an evening.

"It would make more sense than me trying to

keep up the place in Wandsworth when I spend most nights at their place. And we all get on together so well."

"Even with... three of you? I'm sorry, I didn't mean to—"

"No, it's fine. I know it's not usual. But it works for me. For us. That's not to say there aren't compromises to be made." And he didn't mean the fight for the bathroom in the mornings, or who was going to hoover, or the ultimate battle for control of the remote. He could see that other people would baulk at the effort of always considering two other points of view, two other's emotional needs, two other calls for attention. Yet Karel felt his shoulders were broad enough to cope—in fact, the three-way dynamic excited him in a way that no other relationship ever had.

"Each to his own." Patrick looked momentarily weary. "I'm doing my best to cope with one lively man, let alone two. Have you lived with someone before?"

Karel shook his head. There had been boyfriends in his life, but none of them had ever been anywhere near an official, live-in partner.

Patrick grinned. "Plenty to get used to, then."

"What are you talking about?" Lee slid into a

chair at the table, obviously considering he was forgiven for any earlier faux pas.

"The trials of living with someone," Patrick said, the light in his eyes belying his stern words.

"It's marvellous!" Lee said excitedly. "Gives you the chance to know someone properly. To relax with them. To concentrate on what they're really like, what their core values are, how much or how little the daily things matter. You can both laugh at jokes, complain at hurts, rant over disappointments. Plan the days ahead, share the days gone past. Build a life together, rather than as separate individuals. To me, it's having a best friend, a life mate, and a lover, all in one. Like a three scoop ice cream actually!"

Patrick and Karel both stared at him. Patrick had gone red.

"Bugger, this is turning out to be my foot-in-mouth day of the century," Lee said, cheerfully unrepentant. "Was that too much information?" He glanced quickly, almost guiltily at Patrick. "Too much sap?"

Patrick shook his head. The look on his face was almost awed. "Poetic," he said softly. "And there can never be too much poetry."

Karel glanced between them. "I'll collect my ice

cream and get on my way," he said quietly, though he wasn't sure either of them was listening. "And… leave you to it."

He smiled to himself on the way out: they still hadn't moved from their seats, though now they were clasping each other's hand.

They really were an awesome couple.

Chapter 9

Things changed for the worse, very suddenly and very inexplicably. Or so it seemed to Karel.

Arriving back at the flat after work one evening, there was no mistaking the tension in the air. Surprising, because Griff was the only one at home, but a sharp vibration hovered in the kitchen, like an argument had just finished, and raised voices were still reverberating. Karel wondered where Leroy was: he didn't think there was a dance shift at the club that night. In fact, he realised Leroy hadn't mentioned the club for several days, and Karel had been so busy at work he hadn't thought to ask how it was going. Still, the guy was allowed a private life of his own, wasn't he?

"Is Leroy at rehearsals?"

Griff scowled. He was washing up saucepans

with a barely controlled fury. Karel suspected he'd washed them all several times already, judging by their squeaky-clean surfaces. "Leroy's not dancing at the club anymore. He's too bloody busy."

"What?" Karel wanted to ask what kept Leroy, Mr. go-with-the-flow, so busy, but something in Griff's manner stopped him. "He'll miss it, won't he? He dances so well."

"We'll all miss it." Griff looked more angry than upset.

"Has he got another job?" The arts festival was starting the next month, and the fixtures booklet had been out on the kitchen counter more than once. Karel wondered if Leroy had found something there to challenge him. "Have you two had words?"

"*Had words?*" Griff scowled even more. "That's all we ever bloody do nowadays."

Karel almost bit his tongue trying to keep his calm. "Do you want to go out and join Leroy?" *Wherever he is.* "I can message him to meet us at—"

"Don't! That'll upset him." Griff sounded genuinely worried. "He'll come back when he wants."

Karel eased himself onto one of the kitchen

stools. His muscles ached for a hot bath, but this was more important. "You don't always have to wait here, you know. You can do what you want, go where you want."

"That's not gonna happen, is it?"

Karel blinked hard at the bitterness in Griff's tone. "What did I say wrong?"

"Shit, it's not you. But I can't go out without him. No point. Even with him, I can only cope with an hour or two. You know that."

Karel did, but tonight—tired and a little impatient—he didn't want to let it go. "Do you suffer from agoraphobia?" He'd seen Griff's nervousness when they went to the club or a bar together. Griff was right: he barely managed more than a couple of hours, and then only with a beer or two inside him. Too many of them, though, and his behaviour deteriorated. Karel and Leroy did all the shopping and errands, and they rarely ate out. It hadn't taken Karel long to realise that it was to do with Griff himself, rather than his high standards as a chef.

"Don't know what it's called. Never fucking asked anyone. I just..." Griff bit hard at his lower lip. "When I first left... the home, it got worse."

"The home?" Karel gently prompted. He knew

Griff had no family around him, but this was new.

"Foster home. It was fine, okay?"

"Okay."

Griff sighed. He folded the tea towel three times until he seemed satisfied with its shape, and then flopped down into the seat beside Karel. "Yeah. I don't talk about it much. They were decent people, but when I turned eighteen I reckoned I was ready to get my own place, and I bloody insisted on it 'til they helped me get a little flat out Romford way. It's just... things got bad after that. Don't know why."

Karel watched Griff's eyes. He knew now when both men were fooling themselves as well as Karel—or trying to. Griff's bid for independence obviously hadn't been what he expected, or could cope with.

"Just before I met Leroy, it got so I could hardly leave the place. Needed my stuff around me, needed to know where everything was. You know? If I went out... I panicked things wouldn't be the same when I got back."

Karel nodded gently.

"Even now, every day, I just want to... be here. This is where I belong." His jaw was set mulishly, but Karel could see the glint of panic in his eyes. "Looking after things. This is what I do best."

"It is." Karel kept his voice gentle. "And when you first met Leroy? How did he help you?"

Griff started laughing, loudly, shockingly. Tears welled in the corners of his eyes.

"Hey. What did I say this time?"

"Look, I'm not saying he wasn't the saving of me. He fucking *was*. I can leave the bloody house now, at least as long as I can always see him, like at the club, at the ice cream shop. As long as I know he's there. But as for *him* looking after *me*..."

Karel waited, intrigued. He'd discovered over the years that silent patience was so often the best way to elicit information.

"When I met Leroy, he'd just started at the Soho community centre, helping out with kids who gave him nothing but backchat and lice. Well, that was at first. He built up that dance class over months, stuck with it, made something of it. They love him there now."

"You first met him there, at the centre?"

"Yeah. When I did come out of that flat in Romford, I'd come here, to Soho. I know the area, I know how to get around without too much exposure." Griff probably didn't even realise how much he revealed of his condition: he was resigned to it. "The centre was running a cookery course at the time, and I'd always been good at that. Plus they gave classes on website maintenance. Leroy helped me out on the crappy old PC they had there. Then we kind of hooked up. We got on well together."

It was the sweetest, most poignant understatement Karel had ever heard from either of them. "And you moved in here?"

Griff's eyes were a little unfocussed, as if he was remembering that time. "He had this great bloody house but hardly used any of it except for a bed and the studio. Even now, if I weren't here, he'd barely sleep. That's the way he is. He dances, he works out, he sleeps. Then starts dancing again. When we met, he was living on cans of beans and energy drinks. He weighed less than he had in his teens. He needed care!"

Karel heard it as clearly as if Griff had said the words aloud. "*He needed* me!" He reached an arm around Griff's waist and hugged him. "Things are so much better for him now, though. For both of you."

Griff snorted. One single tear eased out of his right eye and ran down his cheek. Karel didn't think he'd even noticed. "You know he was offered an audition at that dance troupe that's in the festival?"

It was a sudden change of subject, but Karel was

used to that with Griff. And it was exactly what he'd had hoped to hear. "That's great, isn't it?"

Griff continued, not really answering to Karel's satisfaction. "He knows a lot of the dancers already in the group. He's helped them out a few times, with rehearsal workshops. A couple of his friends dropped in at the community centre, checking in with him. It'd be a proper contract. With pay! The group's getting a name for themselves, all across London. They give shows in Covent Garden, you know."

"Wow."

"I know, right?" Griff was as puffed up with pride as if he were the dancer himself. "They want him on their training programme too, they've seen how good he is as a teacher."

"So, is he there now?" Karel would love to see Leroy established in a genuine performing group, reaching a bigger audience. More than that, he would love to see Leroy share his enthusiasm and love of dance. He would blossom, Karel could imagine that so vividly.

"He won't do it. I thought he would, he gave up his job at the club, said he'd go to the audition." Griff pushed his glasses up his nose with some kind of venom, even though they immediately bounced back down again. "But he still hasn't been. I told him... well, I told him he's a fucking idiot to pass this up."

That explained the fractious atmosphere in the flat. Where the hell had Karel been, that he'd missed all this going on with the other two? He was disgusted with himself. "But why won't he do it?"

"Parents." Griff shrugged.

Karel felt he was in a strange Twilight Zone. "I'm sorry? He said his mother was pleased he was dancing."

"Oh, don't get me wrong, she loves him, she's pleased he's a dancer. But she's a bloody star. Wedded to her career, was dancing before she could walk. And his dad? He's world famous. They've done a real number on him, that's what."

"Griff," Karel said, as slowly and as calmly as he could. He still hugged Griff but a little more firmly. "It's not fair on me if I don't know what's relevant. I need to know what you're talking about. What matters to you and Leroy. Don't hide things from me."

Griff frowned. "I don't do that. Do I? I mean, I'm used to things being just me and Leroy."

Karel suspected the two men were used not just to each other's company, but to each other's inability to discuss things in the open, but he held his counsel for the moment. "Please explain."

"The gymnastics were part of the plan for him to be a star like she is. Like his dad is, in the classical music world. Then, when he started growing into a less athletic build, and wanted to swap over to dancing... well."

Karel still didn't really understand. His parents hadn't always "got" him, he knew that. They were of a different generation; they were different people altogether. They'd struggled occasionally with his love of art, when no one in the family had ever taken a purely creative path before, and then with his decision to follow Ada to England, because they lost close touch with two of their children. They had also struggled with his coming out, but that had been a long time ago, in his teens, and the shock was much less than his táta—his dad—discovering Karel's football allegiance to Arsenal as opposed to the family's eager following of Manchester United on their crappy old TV back in the old Czechoslovakia.

Yet whatever the struggle, they all knew they loved each other, unconditionally.

"Do you know how driven those bloody ballet dancers are? She made it pretty clear early on that unless Leroy gave up his whole life to it, he'd never make her standard."

"But he's marvellous. He cares so much about it."

"Yeah, right? It's more or less all he wants to do. He never wanted to be a star, to be the very best. He just wanted to dance and have fun. But she didn't understand he just wanted to live here, do his classes, find his own way, be..."

"With you."

"And now, you," Griff said in an almost-whisper.

Karel wouldn't think of that now.

"But he doesn't think he's good enough. Like his Mama used to say. When of course he is!" Griff snapped then winced. "Sorry. It's not your fault. I mean, I tell him, time and again. If he'd just take the audition, he'd realise how good he really is. What he can offer."

Karel took a deep breath. There was so much more to this than he'd imagined.

"And of course, I'm too needy to be of any help to him, right?"

Jesus. "What do you mean? You go out with us both. You just said—"

"No." Griff wriggled in his arms and Karel wasn't sure if it was to escape or to settle closer. "It's stressful every time. I can feel Leroy tense beside me, waiting for me to freak out, or conscious of getting me back home at a moment's notice."

"He loves you," Karel said simply.

The light in Griff's eyes was magical to see: it turned on like the Regents Street Christmas display. "He's a fucking idiot. And I love him too. And he needs things I can't give him, because I can't be with him."

"What does he need, Griff?"

Griff looked up at him then, his expression fierce as it so often was. "He needs his men. Though God knows if that's enough."

Things weren't right. Karel just didn't know what to do about it.

Only the next night, again returning late from work, Karel was caught unawares by his other lover. Leroy was standing in the doorway to the living room, in a suit. In a *suit*.

"Jesus!" Karel said in shock. Leroy looked absolutely marvellous, the jacket hanging elegantly from his shoulders, the trousers snug around his legs. The dark charcoal fabric was perfect against his skin.

But. *A suit?*

"Did you have a business meeting?" he asked. He didn't like to ask if Leroy was off to a wedding or a funeral.

Leroy looked both shifty and annoyed. "A job. I've got a job, working in that new clothes store on Tottenham Court Road. Started yesterday." He ripped his tie out from under his collar with particular harshness.

"A shop?" Karel didn't want to sound like an interrogator, but what the hell was going on? "But you had a job. Though Griff told me you're not dancing at the club anymore."

"Bloody tattle-tail." Leroy shrugged awkwardly out of his jacket and threw it over the back of the sofa. "Don't hassle me. It wasn't making enough money, and I'll be too fucking tired to rehearse after the hours the store's signed me in for. So I gave it up. You understand how things are, Karel, when security's at stake. Food before dance, right?"

Karel was too stunned to be offended at Leroy turning his own words back on him. "I'm sorry, I never thought to ask what you were doing for money."

"Why should you?" Leroy bit his lip. "I told you, we only have to find food and heating and stuff, and we've always managed with my dance money and the bits that Griff can earn. I had savings, too—"

"You've been living on your savings?"

Leroy flushed. "Over the last year, the money they pay me at the club has gone down—everyone's suffering recession nowadays. And Griff... well, he does less and less. So yeah, like I know it's stupid and short-term thinking, but we've been using the savings, and now... they're almost gone."

"Do your parents know?" Karel winced as he heard the words aloud: he hadn't meant to insult.

"I'm not a kid." Leroy's eyes sparked with anger. "And they don't have anything left they can send me. Mum's whole life is the ballet, but it's not like they pay her the kind of wage she can send home to her wayward son for groceries. And she supports Dad, too, he travels with her. He can write scores wherever he is, but it's never been a job with regular earnings. So that doesn't leave any surplus for me. Mum's given me the use of the flat, and keeps it legal, but otherwise? I'm expected to make my own way."

Karel was still parsing things. He always *had* made his own way, but he was appalled that he'd just assumed the two men were earning enough in salary to support the household—at least, that Leroy was. And Karel had been staying at theirs, using the place as if it were his own, contributing little beyond the occasional meal and pot of ice cream.

By now, Leroy had wrenched open his trousers and let them drop where he stood. It was as if he couldn't bear wearing the restrictive clothes a moment longer than necessary. He was already down to a T-shirt and a pair of thigh length briefs. To Karel, that was more Leroy's normal wear than the couture.

"Tell me," he said. It seemed he was always peeling information from them these days, like pulling teeth. "Tell me what's going on here."

"Look." Leroy threw himself down onto the sofa and ran his hand through his hair, the tangles snagging on his knuckles. "We're just about surviving here, man. It wasn't so bad when we first moved in, when Griff had a job in a hotel."

"He's had a full time job before? But I thought—"

"It didn't last," Leroy said, his tone brutal. "Don't get me wrong—"

Karel seemed to be hearing that a lot.

"—he's the best chef I ever knew. Genius talent

when it comes to food! Everyone who worked with him said so. He just couldn't cope with being in a busy kitchen, all those other staff. So he left. Nowadays, he sells an article now and then to a catering magazine, or does occasional consulting gigs for other chefs. He's a bloody good mentor, if they let him work from here. And there's some advertising revenue from the blog."

"That doesn't sound like it's either regular or lucrative," Karel said carefully. This whole conversation felt like walking on eggshells. "Can he consider working outside the house again? Sounds like he'd be welcome anywhere in catering."

Leroy shook his head vigorously. "No can do. You see how he is."

"Surely he'll have to." Karel's patience was starting to wear thin. He'd worked all his adult life, and not always in places he liked. He struggled with the realisation of just how different Leroy and Griff were. "If he wants you both to live well."

"Look, no one wants that more than he does. No one loves me more than he does!" Leroy was increasingly distressed. "You don't know what I was like when we first met..."

"He has mentioned some things to me."

"Yeah? Right. Well. He dragged me up by my

bootstraps when I was at my worst, you know? Made this a proper home. But he was struggling too. He'd lost that hotel job, couldn't get unemployment benefit because he wouldn't take any of the other jobs they'd offer him, and was too proud to go on invalidity. He didn't know what to do next, where to go. Dammit, the first night I met him at the centre, he was bashing away on that ancient PC, trying to write down his recipes, trying to make something happen for himself. Man looked lost, you know?"

Karel remembered Griff's anguished frustration in the kitchen the other night. "I know."

"I only got him back here on the pretext of being too drunk to make it on my own. Griff and public transport... man. You can imagine what a battle that was." He shuddered as if jesting, but Karel could see the strained hurt in his eyes. "He never left me again, Karel. And I don't want him to! He's getting better all the time, now, he'll come to the club with me now, he'll go shopping with me."

"But he can't work outside the house."

Leroy winced. "So, I can do that for us both, right? Like I am, right now."

"Yes. But that should be in something that uses your talents. I heard about the offer from the dance group."

"He told you that, too, did he? Did I say, tattle-tail? The group... It's not my kind of thing, man."

"It's exactly your kind of thing."

He was bickering with Leroy, he could hear the petulance in their voices, like he used to hear from the little nieces and nephews Karel and Ada had left behind.

"Nah. It's a professional company. They want proper dancers."

"Jesus. They want *you*! And you're a proper dancer. What's so hard to accept?"

Leroy didn't answer. His gaze was on the sofa seat beside him rather than meeting Karel's. "Fuck. He's selling his stuff."

"Who is? What stuff?" Karel sat down beside him, his knee pressing close to Leroy's half-bare thigh.

Leroy picked up an opened, padded envelope thrown onto the cushion beside him. The address had been scribbled out and a sheet of plain paper was half attached. Griff had been re-using the cookbook packaging for something. "Griff's foster family was great for him, you know? They loved him... still do. He should never have moved out, though that means I might not have met him. They gave him lots of stuff to get started in his catering career—pans, good knives, gadget stuff I don't even know how to turn on, let alone create meals with. And now... looks like he's selling it to keep us going."

"Fuck this," Karel snapped.

Leroy just nodded. He looked as tearful as Griff had done the previous day.

Karel leaned back in his seat with a deep, slow breath. His mind was in turmoil. These weeks he'd spent with Leroy and Griff were proving to have been misleading at best, at worst a lie. Yet maybe not intentionally. He needed to get a firm handle on the real situation. "Let me get some proper facts about the flat."

"You're safe here, don't worry."

Karel shook his head. That wasn't what he meant, and Leroy should bloody well know it. "I can be trusted," he said, because he didn't assume they would instinctively know that, even by now. "I don't judge. I'm not worried for myself. I'm only asking in case you've been threatened by bailiffs."

Leroy seemed to hunch even further in on himself. "We'll manage. It's fine."

"It's not!" Karel burst out, so angrily that Leroy flinched. "You're being naïve, Leroy. I'll pay a proportion of the bills from now on."

"Jesus, like we're after you for your money—"

"I know you're not! But I should pay my way. I spend almost as much time here as I ever did in my own flat."

"You can't pay for two places, man."

"I'll manage."

"You won't. I mean, you don't need to. You should move in with us." For the first time, Leroy fully met his eyes.

"Griff asked me the same, some time ago."

"See? We both want it. And it's nothing to do with the fucking money. We want this to be your *home*, not the place you just come to for a shag."

"I don't just—!"

"—I'm joking, man." Leroy clasped his arm and slung his leg over Karel's lap. "I know you don't. You wanna be here with us for, like, ever." He said it with a silly sing-song accent, but the truth was all over his expression and in his clinging, craving touch.

Things were a mess. A horrible mess.

"I must be honest with you," Karel said slowly.

"Yeah. Right. You're desperate for it." Leroy gave a slow, lascivious wink.

Karel laughed, though sadly. "Yes, I am. That's

what the two of you do to me. But I told Griff I wanted something more than shagging. So, I'll tell you the same."

"I know that," Leroy said softly. "Didn't I say?"

"I want to think about all this," Karel said. It was as if he were listening to someone else speaking. "I want to work out what's best. And for all of us, not just myself."

For a moment, Leroy's eyes seemed to dampen. Then he leaned into Karel, his lips ghosting on Karel's neck. "And that, man, is why you're here. Why I love you. Why we both do."

Why we both love you. Did Leroy know what he'd just said?

"You're good for us," Leroy continued. "We wanna give you what you need, too. Take all the time you want. But we know already. You belong here with us. We know how good it can be."

Karel's whole body responded in a second. Leroy was perched on his lap, his slender body in Karel's arms, and nothing had ever felt so right. "I know it's good. I know it's fun."

"Don't you see, it's already more than just shagging?"

But, no. Karel didn't. Not at that moment.

He wasn't sure he dared.

Chapter 10

Over the course of the next couple of weeks, Karel was forced to realise that there were times he feared going to the flat as much as he craved it.

Griff was full of tension, like a ball of elastic bands waiting for the outermost one to be snipped, which would release the whole damn lot in a burst. He snapped at them both, he laughed too loudly, he dashed to answer the front door at all hours, before Leroy or Karel could offer to go. Karel assumed the visitors were parcel couriers.

Leroy hated his retail job with a rare passion. On the nights he worked long or late opening hours, the sex between them all would be hard, fast, and angry. It was damned hot, and passions were always high, but it wasn't what Karel wanted as a secure base for his life.

And yet... with them, he was still, and often, the happiest he'd ever been.

Leroy and Griff never went to the club anymore. Karel knew, because he still dropped in there occasionally to see friends. Everyone asked after Leroy. When would he be back? The punters loved to look at him—even though Griff had protested no one appreciated Leroy's performance enough—and the management wanted him back because he drew in the punters.

Karel knew Leroy wanted to dance publicly again. Sometimes he'd wake in the night to find Leroy gone from the bed. Karel knew where he'd be—he'd pad along the corridor quietly, listening to the thud of bare feet on the studio floor, as Leroy twisted and thrust his way through private routines he created to try and keep himself in shape.

He'd heard Leroy slump to the floor and cry privately, too.

Meanwhile, Griff progressed to days when he would barely speak. The freezer was full of multi-portioned meals that Karel couldn't see them ever finishing, even if they were a band of twelve, let alone the trio they were: two men barely eating, and the third becoming nothing more than a visitor.

And almost all the sophisticated kitchen equipment had mysteriously vanished.

Karel dragged himself back and forth to work, his mind a mess, but glad of a job that kept his hands occupied. What was worse, he began to feel like the pig in the middle. They didn't put him there deliberately, but too often he found himself caught between cheering up Leroy and calming down Griff. After realising the financial pressures Griff and Leroy were under, he'd taken over paying for the utilities at the flat, because at least then the place would be warm and well lit. Leroy could still dance in comfort, and Griff could cook all the hours he needed.

Karel worked longer hours on site, took some extra private jobs. Yet it was only ever a temporary fix. What was he to do?

Was this even his damned problem?

The other two had managed before he met them, they'd manage again.

They weren't stupid.

He could leave.

No!

It had been a gradual, almost reluctant epiphany for him, but he knew now that he loved Leroy and

Griff—both individually, and as a unit. It had crept up on him, twisting his lust and fascination into something that was deeper and more committed— and a hell of a sight more confusing. And why so painful? All he wanted was to be with them, yet he knew with every shred of common sense he still clung to that he couldn't survive the anguished, volatile atmosphere their current position created.

He remembered *A Tale of Two Cities*, a book he'd once read in school. "It was the best of times, it was the worst of times." Never had a quotation felt so apt. There was so much fun and compassion and loyalty between them—yet so much disorientation and misery. And how long before even his money wasn't enough to keep them all in basic comfort?

For the time being, he treasured the quieter evenings, when Leroy had time off from work and Griff was calm. When they sat together in front of the TV, or shared a meal, or messed about playing one of the old board games Griff still had a supply of in a living room cupboard.

Like tonight.

"I win," Griff announced boldly after hopping his counter across the board according to some convoluted arcane rule that Karel hadn't even bothered to try and understand.

"You cheat," Leroy retorted, lying on his stomach on the rug beside the low table they were playing on.

"You're just a jealous dog."

"You're just an immoral pig."

Karel laughed, enjoying the banter, the flirting, the not-so-casual touches between them. It seemed their love had been stretched too thinly recently. He was sitting on the floor at the base of the sofa, opposite the two of them, not entirely comfortable but too tired to bother moving.

Griff nudged Leroy's shoulder and tilted his head towards Karel. "Watch us," he said playfully to Karel.

"I've been doing that for the last hour," Karel protested. "Else how would I know just how *much* you cheat?"

Griff chuckled, then rolled down onto the rug beside Leroy and drew him into a long, messy kiss.

Karel loved to watch: it was almost as good as joining in. *Almost.* Who knew that voyeurism would turn out to be a private pleasure of his? Leroy and Griff were fabulous together, and yet when they were making out, or even fucking, at no time did they exclude Karel from the delight. They would talk to him, break away to kiss him, play a role for him to direct, display themselves as if he was the sole, VIP spectator—and he would relax in his chair or in the bed, stroking gently at the front of his jeans as they played.

Tonight was going to be one of those nights. He settled against the sofa frame and eased out his legs. A shove on the edge of the table moved it out of his line of vision, so he could clearly see the other two men on the floor.

Leroy's lips found Griff's with familiar passion, his mouth trailing caresses over Griff's face and neck. Karel knew how that felt: he knew how good Leroy was at finding the most sensitive areas. Griff growled his pleasure and ran his hands down Leroy's hips. It made Leroy arch, another of his catlike responses.

They're gorgeous.

Karel had always found them an exotic, erotic couple. But now he'd joined their lives, his feelings were richer, more assured. There was no envy when he saw them together, except in as far as he wanted a taste of it. And he knew that would be available for him, when he needed to join in. For now, for this evening, he wanted to be the observer.

They smiled, they kissed. Karel listened to the soft but sloppy sounds of their breath, the occasional low gasp or laugh. Leroy peeled Griff's shirt up over his head, and then tugged his sweats down. With delight, Karel saw that Griff wasn't wearing underwear: his cock bounced out over the waistband to lie plump on his pale-skinned thigh. Leroy did his usual snake-wriggling trick to shed his clothes and slid down Griff, naked, trailing his darker fingers down the hairs on Griff's body, from chest to belly to pubes. His mouth followed the trail, his tongue licking the skin as if seeking and savouring individual drops of sweat, until his lips docked over Griff's cock. Griff groaned and his cock thickened in Leroy's mouth: Karel could see the bump against the inside of Leroy's cheek. Griff's hips lifted and he started to thrust in and out.

Leroy hummed with excitement, as if singing around his mouthful. Griff grunted with satisfaction, grabbed Leroy's hair, and anchored himself firmly against Leroy's face as they rocked together. They loved going down on each other and—to be fair—also on Karel.

Things were different tonight, though. Things seemed... awkward.

Griff glanced over at Karel many times. Even Leroy's gaze angled up through his sweaty lashes, over to where Karel sat. Their passion was indisputable and damned hot to view, but it didn't hide the insecurity in their eyes, the occasional clumsiness of their hands. Griff was still angry at life: Leroy in misery.

Karel pulled up onto his knees, his hand stroking the front of his own sweats, where his erection ached with need. He wanted to join them—he wanted to reassure them—but he stayed where he was, just watching. They bucked, panting, suddenly fierce. Leroy's leg jerked, stubbing his toe on the edge of the table, and when Griff threw out a hand, his knuckles whacked hard on the rim of a discarded beer bottle. In other circumstances, they would have laughed about all that.

Not tonight.

Karel could read the discontent like subtitles on a TV programme. Could read *them*. Even as they came, almost together but not quite, the climax wasn't properly satisfying: wasn't conclusive. When they rolled apart, there wasn't the usual tangle of hugs and play-slaps and post-coital chuckles. Somehow they blamed each other for the disorientation, yet seemed to have no idea how to pull themselves out of the mess they were in.

Sex had always been the easiest, happiest, most

collaborative thing of all. But now... It hurt, too, even if it was only emotionally. Karel wanted things to be good again, to enjoy this life they had, this understanding, this love—but not a single one of them was happy as it was.

How the hell were they going to make that happen for all three?

Karel didn't argue much himself. He felt things deeply, but argument was wasted effort and emotion, in his opinion. But he had recent experience of the way Leroy and Griff fought, and with the current tension in the flat, a simple, misdirected comment could be a powder-keg. Tonight, the raised voices in the kitchen alerted him to the fact that something had blown up again.

It was the night after the awkward sex session, and he was in the living room, standing on a chair to fix a light fitting that wasn't working. Leroy had been working another late night and the early evening had been quiet without his presence. Griff had left the kitchen almost immediately after supper with Karel and, as far as Karel knew, had hidden himself somewhere in the bedroom with

Karel's laptop. He must have come back into the kitchen when Leroy returned.

By the time Karel had screwed the bulb back in safely and climbed down off the chair, they were yelling. Griff and Leroy bantered loudly, and often, but this was a different scale entirely.

"You know I bloody would if I could!" That was Griff.

"Then do it!"

"Fucking can't—"

"Then get off *my* fucking back, it's the same as me going to the dance group."

"It's fucking *nothing* like it! That'd be good for you, it's what you really want, an audience—"

"And you don't want that, too? Like a better place to cook, an audience of diners apart from us? Don't lie to me. But hey, that's all you bloody do nowadays—"

"And all you do is *weep*! You think we don't hear you? And when I try to help, you just don't wanna know!"

Karel ran along the corridor as fast as he could, but even so, he was shocked at the scene in front of him. Griff and Leroy stood a couple of feet apart, both solid with tension, bodies shaking and faces red, both mouths wide and set in an ugly twist of pain and anger.

Griff held a small paring knife in his hand. Karel wasn't sure why or how he knew to move swiftly—he didn't believe Griff wished him or Leroy any harm with it, and it was too small to inflict anything but a superficial cut without serious intent—but there was something in the furious grip of Griff's fist that scared him. A glance at Leroy's face saw a similar sliver of fear in among the anger. Not enough to make Leroy back away, but enough to make Karel step between them. He took hold of Griff's wrist, removed the blade, and then drew Griff into a hug.

Griff was as stiff as a board for at least half a minute, unresisting, unresponsive, in Karel's arms. Then suddenly, it was as if that virtual elastic band broke inside him and he went limp.

"What the hell are you fighting about?" Karel demanded.

"I can't do it. He knows I can't. You think I wouldn't, if I could?" It was a jumble of tearful words, and Griff was shaking now.

"Hush," Karel said. It was all he could think of to say.

"You'd think I was pimping him out to slave traders," Leroy said, his voice brutal with barely suppressed contempt. "Just get a job! That's all he needs to do. Like the fucking rest of us."

"Enough," Karel warned him. "We can't talk about it while you're both like this. We'll sort out the money situation somehow between us."

"Nothing to sort out," Leroy snapped. He'd gripped the edge of one of the kitchen stools: his knuckles were whitening fast. "And it's not all about money."

"Of course not."

"But it bloody helps," Leroy said, gaze firmly on Griff.

"Fuck off," Griff said. "So, how's that *job* working out for you?" He wrestled away from Karel's grasp and grimaced as if it were all a joke, but there was no humour in his eyes, and the words had a sharp, grim edge. Yet Karel had a feeling Griff directed the sharpness at himself, not Leroy.

"At least I leave the goddamn house!"

"Yes, to ponce about in a suit for rich tourists and their mastercards, wasting yourself on people who don't give a shit about you!"

For a moment, Leroy looked horribly pained. "While you mop and dust everything to within an inch of its fucking life, when we're the only ones who ever see it!"

"*When* you're bloody home to see it, and when's *that* nowadays?"

"We have to eat, you arsehole, we all do, don't we—!"

"Stop it," Karel shouted. "Stop it!"

Shocked, they both fell silent. Karel deliberately let go of Griff and stepped away from the kitchen counter. He found himself in the middle of them—how appropriate was that?—with both men little more than an arm's length away.

"Karel." Leroy held his arms out as if in supplication. "Come to me."

"Fuck everything." Griff frowned but he, too, turned to Karel. His expression cleared when his troubled eyes met Karel's. "I want you," he said.

It was as if they conspired to tug him apart.

"No," Karel said. His voice didn't sound like his own. "No."

The last thing he saw was the look of shock and distress on their startled faces as he turned and walked steadily out of the flat.

Chapter 11

It would be amusing how often people ended up at *With A Kick* when they were thinking through a problem, if it wasn't so true.

Patrick sat down opposite Karel at one of the tables by the window, depositing two large mugs of tea in front of them. Karel knew Patrick had made them personally because they weren't the smaller, smarter cups the shop used for customers. Patrick had often made tea for the workmen when the shop was being rebuilt: Lee had, as well. At least, when Patrick and Lee hadn't been alternately smooching or misunderstanding each other in their torturous path to true romance.

Those seemed much simpler days to Karel, at

least in memory. He glanced around the café as he took a hearty drink. "It looks good. Did I say that already?"

Patrick politely didn't reply, but of course, Karel *had* said it already, on many previous visits. But today, that was all the conversation Karel had found for the last ten minutes as he sat in the mercifully quiet shop in what felt like utter bewilderment.

"I think the place is almost better for the disaster," Patrick replied. "I'd never liked the wall between the kitchen and the café. It's much brighter now with the archway between. And the windows had needed replacement for a long time." He sat quietly for a while, stirring his tea carefully, though Karel didn't remember Patrick ever taking sugar in his drinks. "And we have so many people to thank for helping us out. I don't think I'll ever repeat myself too much on *that*. Thanks for the work you did."

"No problem."

"And I like having you as a customer."

"Yeah, Sure."

"But I think... you're not here just for the ice cream."

Karel glanced down at his bowl. Patrick had been half-teasing, he could tell, but that didn't excuse the fact that the ice cream he'd ordered when he arrived had almost melted into a cold puddle of three swirled colours and flavoured gin. He'd only taken a couple of mouthfuls. "You're an excellent ice cream designer, Patrick. It's not personal."

Patrick chuckled. "I don't take it as such, believe me."

Karel still stared at the bowl, but his thoughts weren't on the dessert. "I thought I wanted it when I came here... then, for some reason, perhaps, I didn't."

Patrick probably suspected Karel wasn't talking only about the ice cream. As soon as Karel had burst into the shop that morning, at an unusual time of day, and unusually flustered, Patrick had left whatever he'd been attending to and come to greet him with calm deliberation and refreshment. Just as a good friend would do. And Karel knew that was exactly what he needed.

Patrick leaned back in his chair as if settling for a while. "I like you, Karel. You were a tower of strength when we were getting the shop back on its feet. And then you became a friend as well."

Karel smiled gently. "When you stopped worrying I would seduce Lee away from you."

"I... yes, well, there was that. I wasn't myself at

that time. "

"I know. And thank you. For the friendship. I treasure it."

Patrick nodded and drank more tea. He winced, as if maybe he hadn't meant to put all that sugar in but had been distracted. "Excuse me for prying, perhaps, but your two men... is that situation like the ice cream, too? You wanted it—"

So badly! Karel's whole gut cramped at the fresh thought of Leroy and Griff.

"—but then, for some reason, you didn't."

Patrick was a dangerous fellow in many ways, Karel thought. Not just because he was a hot bear, and served fabulous ice cream, but because he was sharp. And, very painfully, kind.

Karel sighed. "I still want it, Patrick. But I'm not sure what *it* is."

"There's been trouble?"

"Just..." Karel wasn't sure how he would describe it. "Yes, there was. And I was a coward. I ran away from them."

"I suspect you'd only do that if you were truly overwhelmed." Patrick also sighed. "It's always a risk, a new relationship, and especially when the guy—or guys—are new to you. It's like setting off on a trip that you're looking forward to, but then

175

you find someone else has packed your luggage and you don't know what you're going to find in it."

The analogy was amusing and somehow calming to Karel's churning, incipient panic.

"Tell me about them," Patrick said. "Your guys."

"It won't change anything."

"Who says it won't?"

Karel shook his head, but he appreciated Patrick's attempts to comfort. "Leroy is... he's magical. He's amused at everything, truly talented. He loves to perform, it makes him glow from within, even if he doesn't always see that on his own behalf. He's loved Griff for a long time, protects him closely. But otherwise, he's very relaxed and laid back, and so very generous with money..." Karel smiled, despite his low thoughtful mood. "And with his affection."

"And after he's given all this attention to others?"

It was a very perceptive comment. "He doesn't seem to have enough reserves left. He doesn't imagine he deserves anything for himself. He doesn't think he's good enough for success."

"And Griff?"

Karel was already feeling better. He wondered absently how Patrick managed to talk about Karel's men as kindly and with the same respect as Karel did himself. "He's strong, yet he thinks he's a failure. He's brutally honest and his loyalty is fierce, having cared for Leroy since the day they met, physically and emotionally. But he struggles with socialising, Patrick. I don't know the last time he left the house on his own. He's built walls around him to keep him safe, and now he's trapped. Yet he has so much care and support to offer."

"To you, too, I imagine."

"Yes, me too." Karel realised how much he'd come to rely on the comfort of a home, of somewhere he could share with the men he loved, that suited them, that welcomed and warmed them at all hours of the day.

"And together?"

"They're a loving couple. They dote on each other. They've supported each other through the worst of times."

"I meant," Patrick said gently. "Together with you."

Karel flushed. "They are... they have difficulties." At that moment, it seemed like the biggest understatement of the century. "The loving is easy for them, I think. It's the living that's tougher to handle."

"That's the same for many of us."

"Yes. I suppose so."

"Yes, it is," Patrick said more firmly. "Doesn't mean anyone is the less for it. Doesn't mean the difficulties can't be dealt with."

Karel smiled. "You talk more like my father than my friend."

"Oh Jesus. Thanks. *Not.*" Patrick rolled his eyes, and they both laughed. Karel picked up his spoon and scooped a little of the mashed ice cream. It still tasted good.

The strains of a country and western ballad filtered through the window, and they both glanced out into the street. A busker was setting up his guitar case, laughing with another young man who was shaking his head, running a hand through his hair. Curtis and Riley. There was another awesome couple.

He wanted that closeness, and it had almost been there—

"Your men need you," Patrick said, breaking into his thoughts.

"My...?" Karel frowned. "No. I mean, I'm not sure about that. They were okay before I came along."

"Doesn't sound like it. I don't want to patronise you or anything, Karel, but it calls to mind something Curtis told me once. When he had that bit of bother with his ex, remember?"

Karel had been told about it: Curtis had always been frank with him. He seemed to consider Karel a fellow spirit, opposed to some of Curtis' younger and more irresponsible friends. Curtis' ex-boyfriend had been abusive to him in the past, and when Curtis escaped the relationship, had threatened him with debt. It had taken a group of Curtis' friends to scare off the ex, once and for all.

"Curtis told me you don't have to take a punch to the jaw to feel beaten up," Patrick said. "A blunt analogy, but Curtis is good at seeing the wood for the trees. He'll call it out, too."

They were both watching Riley strumming his guitar. Curtis threw his hands in the air as if Riley wasn't listening to whatever creative advice Curtis was giving him. Yet they were both still grinning in that way that couples have, over a fond, private joke.

"Like I said," Patrick continued. "It sounds like Leroy and Griff need you. Be gentle with them. It's not always easy to sort out your own problems when you're swamped under a shit-pile of them."

"I'm not their parent," Karel said, rather too sharply. It wasn't his way to be petulant, but it had been a very trying week. "Nor their counsellor. I don't have any magic bullet solutions."

"I know. But you have the motivation and the compassion to try. And maybe to see things more clearly than they can. In your relationship, you'll be the one to see the wood for the trees, and the wood? It's whatever you want to come of this."

There was further disturbance outside. Curtis was hugging a tall, slender, black man, and clasping hands with another, plumper, white man wearing glasses.

"They're here," Karel said. His heart swelled, plummeted, then rose again. They'd followed him—or maybe just come looking by chance. Did he care how or why? *They're here*.

Patrick stood slowly, pushing his chair back under the table as if he knew Karel would be on his way shortly. "If you want me to talk to them...?"

"No. It's something I must do myself." But Karel smiled up at his friend, because, yes, Patrick had given him food for thought and valuable perspective. "Something they need me to do."

"Good for you," Patrick said. "But remember to include what *you* want, in whatever you do. Be gentle with yourself, as well."

They'd ambushed him, but they didn't come into *With A Kick*. They stayed outside on the pavement, close together, occasionally touching a hand, or nudging a shoulder. They seemed to be engrossed in each other, but Karel saw how they would glance through the shop window every few seconds, as if they couldn't resist looking for him. He took another couple of mouthfuls of ice cream while he gathered his thoughts, then walked outside to join them.

"I wanted to come and see you," Leroy said quietly. "To explain things." He had to step off the kerb as a group of tourists shuffled past, then nearly collided with a passing pushbike.

To the sound of an angry bike bell, Karel took a hand from each of them and moved all three men back under the shop awning. People still passed them by—and he wondered if they'd be entertainment for the remaining customers inside—but the wall was cool at his back and the street sounds were muted, and it reduced the risk of them being parted at a moment's whim.

"I just want you to come back," Griff said, more bluntly. He'd relaxed a little as soon as they moved away from the traffic. "So, I said I'd come with

Leroy, but he said it'd be too much. That you were intimidated by us. By the couple thing."

"Jesus, man." Leroy rolled his eyes at Griff. "Shut up and let me speak as we planned, will ya?"

"I'm not intimidated," Karel said. "Not in the way you think." It was like the time he first met them. They fidgeted, they bantered, they tried to touch each other—and him—every moment. They were both ridiculous and adorable together.

"Anyway. We came to see you together," Leroy said. His voice was ragged. "Because we are together, we don't deny it."

"We don't want to."

"I know." Karel *did* know: none of this was news. None of this was the problem in his eyes, either. "You're good together."

"I love him. I know he needs to be home. I didn't mean to bully him," Leroy said, and Karel heard a thread of panic in his voice.

"Stupid bastard," Griff said, but his hand tightened on Leroy's. "Love you too. Didn't mean to drop shit on your job, I know you're doing what you can. The sun shines out of your bloody arse for me."

Leroy turned back to Karel, his eyes wide and needy. "So. That's how it is with us."

"I know," Karel repeated. He wasn't sure what was happening here. He agreed with everything they said: they seemed to have found a reconciliation for the moment. But where was he to stand in all this? "And that's how it should be. I understand."

"But you don't!"

"Fuck," Griff said directly, and maybe too loudly—a passing jogger in neon yellow lycra startled, then swerved over to the other side of the street. "We're shit at explaining, that's what it is. No wonder we're in such trouble."

"We've been so much better with you. We've been happier. Steadier."

"Better," Griff repeated, as forcefully if he wrestled the word to the ground and beat it into submission. "But that's not enough for you, is it?"

What could Karel say? Here they were, in front of him, the two men he'd come to need and want like nothing and nobody else.

"What do you think I want?" he asked. "To be your arbiter? To settle troubles between you—to balance your silly arguments? I'm a man in my own right."

Leroy shook his head furiously. "We know. We know. That's not what I want."

"Me neither." Griff was rubbing gently up against Karel again, as if he needed the physical reassurance.

"We want you to have our love and support, too. The love goes both ways." Leroy swallowed hard. "I think maybe we forgot that."

"So, what's to do?" Griff's determined tone had a thread of despair too. "We need to sort it all out, pretty damn quick."

Leroy's laugh was wearier than usual. "Fucked if I know how. I've only ever lived with you, Griff, and I seem to mess that up all the time."

"We want to make it right." Griff nodded, frowning, then nodded again. *Make it so*, he seemed to imply, though he looked as bemused as Leroy.

And that was the final breakthrough. Guidance came to Karel like its own kind of emotional missile. *The loving is easy for them: it's the living that's tougher to handle*. They wanted to make things work. He, Karel, had been the one keeping them at bay. There were few things they couldn't put right if they pitched in together.

"Like the ice cream," he said aloud.

"Huh?"

"Top and Tails," Karel said, He felt a little light-headed. "Three scoops individually tasty, but more delicious as a mixture."

"Are you on something?" Griff peered at him. "Gonna share?"

Leroy thumped Griff on the arm. "Leave him be. He's channelling something from the great space-time continuum."

Karel laughed. God, it was good to laugh! Leroy gave a broad grin and Griff's eyes sparkled with glee behind his lenses. "You, Leroy."

"Yessir?"

Karel ignored the flippancy. "You must stop the shop job. Go for the audition with the dance group."

"What the fuck? I can't... I mean." He looked in some panic at Griff. "I told you, I'll get around to it, probably, maybe—"

"This week. I'll go with you," Karel interrupted. The decisive tone in his voice was a revelation, even to him. "And Griff?"

Griff blinked hard. "I want to work, you know? I know I'm useless stuck in the flat. I'll find something."

Karel shook his head dismissively. "You're far from useless. But you must stop cooking, for God's sake. I cannot eat that much fettucine, even with that sinfully good basil pesto sauce you make. We'll think about jobs you might do, but that also suit you. Yes, we'll find something."

Griff shook his head doubtfully, but his eyes gleamed with something that looked like hope. "You're a bossy bastard, you know?"

"But our bossy bastard," Leroy teased, and there was only a tiny question mark at the end of it.

"I want to help you both. Help us all."

"You already do," Leroy said softly. He linked his arm into Karel's: his eyes briefly fluttered closed and his moistened lips parted. It was the equivalent of a full on snog.

"I was a coward," Karel said, just as softly. He put his hand over Leroy's and used his other arm to gather Griff into his side. "I left you when you were struggling."

"Man, we're all cowards." Leroy sighed.

"Yes, but—"

"You'll come back?" Griff interrupted, his tone impatient and needy.

That's just the way I love them. Karel nodded, smiling.

It was only as they turned to head back to the Tube that Karel realised Curtis and Riley were still only a few feet away. Riley was concentrating on his singing—it may have been an Ed Sheeran cover, it may have been something from *Thomas the Tank Engine*, Karel couldn't tell in amongst the western twang—but Curtis caught his eye, with a grin that confirmed he'd heard some of what Karel and the others were discussing.

And as Karel frowned at him to keep his distance, Curtis just gave him a huge, leery wink.

Chapter 12

Karel was damned well going to make this work.

The following evening, he found a quiet place in the bedroom and fired up Skype. He wouldn't be disturbed for a while—Leroy had started dancing back at the club, and Griff was in the process of dismantling his Ebay account and looking for other ways to monetise his blog.

Now Karel needed to move things forward.

Skype rang, the circling hoop shrank away, and Ada's face appeared, a big grin on her face. "Hi, *bratříček*." She smiled but her carefully darkened brows dipped in a frown. "What's up?"

"Cut to the chase, why don't you?" Frightening, how well she could read him. "Do you still dance, big sis?"

Ada blinked, startled. "Only in clubs. I've always

been too busy to start classes again. Let's face it, the Royal Ballet haven't been knocking on my door, have they?"

He smiled: she was being modest, though she'd certainly never be Leroy's standard. "That's not the point, I think."

"I... no. It isn't, you're right." Her expression softened. "I love dancing, regardless."

"Would you consider attending a kind of masterclass this week? In this part of London, at a private studio. It's nothing sinister, I'll be there as well."

Ada frowned again, but in mischief now. "Is this something to do with your new man?"

"One of them."

"One of...? Oh, *really*?"

"I'll explain another time," he said, enjoying her frustrated eyebrow-waggling. "But for now, he needs a pupil who can respond on an adult level to him, who can reassure him he's a good teacher."

Ada never suggested that maybe Karel's guy *wasn't* a good teacher—she was a good *sestra*. She trusted her brother.

"I'd be glad to," she said. "Actually, I'm free tomorrow, if that's not too short notice. On one condition—"

"No," he said quickly, though he laughed happily with her. "Absolutely no details on who sleeps where in the bed!"

A couple of days later, Karel went with Leroy to the audition. He didn't know what he'd expected at the dance group's studio around the back of St Martin's Lane. A room full of slender, wispy, graceful creatures, maybe, whose steps made butterfly movements, who held their heads high and their gaze distant. Elegant hand gestures, undistracted commitment, shockingly limber bodies...

Well, there was all that, but also a bunch of raucous, boisterous young people—and a few older ones, too—who sang, shouted laughter, and shoved each other with cheery carelessness. A group by the door, who were apparently also waiting on an audition, broke into a pastiche of disco dancing at a moment's notice. In another, distant rehearsal room, Karel could hear the distant strain of a karaoke version of Abba hits. Considering it was only days before the festival started and performances were due to begin, he was bemused and confused as to how they'd ever create a cohesive group in time.

Yet he really enjoyed himself, watching and marvelling at the enthusiasm and exhibitionism, while he waited for Leroy to emerge from a small practice room. Occasionally a dancer would smile flirtatiously at him, which he had to admit was flattering. And on one occasion he left his uncomfortable plastic bucket seat to help a couple of girls carry a rolled-up backdrop curtain along the hallway.

When Leroy appeared again, he was grinning and shaking hands with someone Karel assumed was a director of the group. They spoke for a while, both of them nodding, and mobile phones were produced as if to fix a date in the calendar. It all looked very encouraging to Karel, not that he'd ever doubted Leroy would be just what they needed. There was something about the vibe in this place that unnerved Karel but settled around Leroy like a suit of comfortable clothes.

Leroy sauntered over, acknowledging greetings from a couple of other dancers, but with his gaze on Karel. He wore a loose, dark red vest, and leggings under a pair of bright green shorts that may have originally been Griff's: the drawstring

191

was wrapped a couple of times around his slender waist. His face was flushed, his movements relaxed and fluid, his eyes sparkling. Karel was hard within seconds, rather embarrassingly so. He shifted on his seat, settling his hands in his lap to hide his response. Bizarre really, when ninety per cent of the people passing through the room at any time were in skimpy tights and leggings that showed every curve of their damned arse.

"Coffee break?" he asked Leroy.

Leroy nodded. He brushed up against Karel as if wanting to touch, but not in company, so Karel led them to an indoor table in a nearby coffee bar.

"So? How did it go?" When Leroy refused cake—he was always partial to pastry, especially Griff's creations—Karel suspected he had his answer: Leroy was already thinking about his training. He clasped Leroy's hand in one of his, the other hand stirring a spoon of sugar into his own latte. "You took the offer, yes?"

"Well, I should officially wait for feedback from the audition—" Leroy caught the look in Karel's eye, and laughed. "Yes, they offered me a place, and this time, I took it."

"You remembered what I said?"

"Yes, coach," Leroy teased.

"Hey. I don't really know anything about dance—"

"No." Leroy twisted his hand to link fingers with Karel's, tight and earnest. "Maybe not, but you told me to imagine I was dancing for you in the studio, at home. You told me that would give me the confidence, would make me shine. You told me it was time to grow the fuck up—"

"I never did!" Karel nearly spluttered his coffee over the tablecloth.

Leroy laughed, very brightly. "Gotcha. But you were right—about everything. I'm very excited about it. They want me to start immediately—do you realise how soon the festival starts, and how under-rehearsed some of the sets are?—and I think there'll be enough time for me to catch up on all the routines."

"And help others with the same thing," Karel murmured, thinking of the happy but hectic chaos he'd seen at the studio. It seemed to me they were a fairly immature group. They needed Leroy to show them some serious discipline.

"Then, after the festival, I can choose my role in the troupe, whether it's solely in performance or with the training classes."

How his eyes sparkled! "I am so very pleased,"

Karel said. "It's such good news for you."

Leroy took a sip of his cappuccino, the froth resting on his upper lip like a coffee moustache.

It took all of Karel's self-restraint to wipe it off with his finger rather than his tongue. "Was it any help, the session with Ada?"

"You know it was." Leroy's cheeks were pink with excitement and pleasure. "She's fun. And a pretty good dancer."

"Not as good as you."

Leroy peered at him, as if he thought Karel might be poking fun, but he wasn't. The session with Ada had happened the day after Karel asked her to help, and before Leroy could find an excuse to avoid it, but luckily he and Ada had hit it off immediately. Karel had been in the flat, as promised, but had left them to dance alone. He surrendered to his curiosity only a couple of times, when he peeked back into the studio. The first time, Ada had been concentrating fiercely on following Leroy's instructions: Leroy had been encouraging and full of motivation, alight with the joy of imparting his knowledge. The second time Karel checked in, the two of them had been in fits of laughter in each other's arms.

He'd only been a tiny bit jealous.

"But I assume that was your plan?" Leroy said, eyes wide over the rim of his coffee cup.

"My plan?"

"Whatever you plotted with your poor innocent sister. And don't roll your eyes like that! It was to build my confidence. To try and show me I had sufficient professional skill, that I could work as both performer and tutor."

"*Try* to show you?" Karel teased back. "Just don't encourage her to pole dance, please." He was only half joking.

"No chance. I don't need more competition. She wants to take up a few private lessons, in fact... if that's okay with you?"

"Why shouldn't it be? It's a great idea. If you have time, of course."

"I'll start after the festival, I'll be too busy while performances are on. But when the group starts another semester of student classes, I'll organise a private schedule as well." Leroy paused and put down his cup. His fingers played with the edge of Karel's plate: there was a slice of Karel's pastry still untouched. "I'll have to talk to Griff about streamlining my diet now I'll be professionally training."

"Start tomorrow," Karel murmured, if only for

the opportunity to feed the final sliver of sticky pastry through Leroy's lips.

"Thank you," Leroy said suddenly.

"For tempting you to put on weight?"

It was Leroy's turn to roll his eyes. "For bullying me, man. It's what I needed. Oh, I know, it's not really bullying. Instead, you sent me Ada and her mad sense of humour and her way of making me feel like I really know what I'm doing."

"Which you always did—"

"Hush. Let me say my piece. And you took a day off work to get me here today, and you stayed to see how it went. And now you're here to celebrate with me and... yeah." He grabbed the morsel of pastry and popped it into his mouth. "To tempt me to put on weight I can ill afford."

Karel laughed. He would love Leroy whatever size the dancer was, but he'd also do what he could to help him keep match fit, as Griff was apt to call it. "You can run rings around me, Leroy, and I'll listen to whatever you want to talk about—but I won't take crap." He gestured at Leroy's body, at his dance gear. "This is you. This is what you must be."

"There's still one issue." Leroy looked suddenly serious. "Maybe I didn't want to face that one, either."

"Tell me."

"The group travels. Usually just around London, but sometimes they tour. They're young, they're learning. They need to broaden their experience. And they want to promote more satellite training groups. I could be involved in that."

"So? If you have to travel, then I'll be here with Griff." Karel didn't say *for* Griff because he wouldn't dream of humiliating his man, but both he and Leroy knew what he meant. "We'll be fine until you get back."

"Karel?" Leroy looked pained for a moment, then gave the broadest smile Karel had ever seen on his face. "God, you're fine."

Karel shook his head, embarrassed—this was nothing, just what Leroy needed, and what he, Karel, could give—and now he was in danger of getting too sentimental for public view. He noticed how Leroy was shifting restlessly now, his gaze darting to the café door. Back in the direction of the studio they'd just left. "You want to stay a bit longer with the group, catch up with the festival programme?"

Leroy was an enchanting mixture of reluctance, relief, and pure delight. "You okay with that? I reckon I need all the time I can get. And there's a student meeting after the auditions, where I'd like to meet some of the new guys."

Karel stood, and they hugged briefly but so, so warmly. "I'll be at home. We'll both be there, for when you finish."

Chapter 13

Karel was sitting in the studio, his back to the mirror, reading one of Leroy's favourite thrillers, when Leroy finally came home around eleven o'clock. Griff had been watching an old movie in the living room, and now Karel listened absentmindedly as the two voices murmured along the hallway, then two sets of footsteps approached to join him.

"Karel? I thought you might be in here. It's the first place we look nowadays." Leroy folded gracefully down to sit beside him, cross-legged. He looked tired, but was still in his dance gear, still smiling, still emotionally energised.

"I'm not avoiding either of you." Karel smiled

back. God, but it was good to see Leroy happy again! "I just like time to unwind sometimes, on my own. And this is a good book you recommended."

"Ada's coming around tomorrow for lunch," Griff announced. He flopped rather than folded onto the floor, and nudged up against Karel's other side. "We're going to plan our diaries so we can all go together to Leroy's performances at the festival. You'll be able to get the time off?"

"Of course." If his workaholic sister could, Karel reckoned he could match her. They were his men before hers, after all.

"Better warn you, it could be interpretive dance, and we'll all be dressed as seaweed. Or the soundtrack will be loud, tortured violins," Leroy teased him. He knew Karel's taste in music was conservative. "Or—alert!—I won't be taking any of my kit off."

"You think that matters?" Karel teased back. He put down the book and cupped Leroy's cheek. "I can see what you've got, any night of the week."

Griff made a soft, growly sigh behind him. His hand slid onto Karel's lap.

"Man." Leroy seemed visibly to relax and reached his face up for a kiss. "Thanks for all you did for me."

"I told you. It's what I want, too." Karel leaned back, comfortable in loose clothing and socks, with his men in his arms, breathing in the quiet air of the room. He was sitting on an old woollen throw that he'd brought with him, firstly to London, now to the flat. His great aunt had knitted one each for him and Ada, while they were both babies. It was full of dropped stitches and snagged seams, but he didn't care. His had a lingering, soft smell to it by now: the smell of all three men.

And wasn't that a new smell all of its own?

Leroy cleared his throat. "But you deserve much more than my thanks—"

"Mine too," Griff murmured.

"—whether you'll ask for it or not. So, we've been doing some plotting of our own."

Karel frowned. "What's going on?"

"You could work here." Leroy gestured expansively around the room, his words halfway between a statement and a question.

"Me? I thought we established I'm no dancer."

"I mean, for your art. Your sculpture. Isn't this enough space for you to bring in the materials you need?"

Karel's heart began beating furiously. He didn't believe you should expect to have everything you wanted, whenever you wanted it. That was why he stayed away from the subject of his art whenever he could.

"You avoid talking about it," Griff said roughly, echoing Karel's thoughts, frighteningly perceptive. "Your art."

Jesus.

"But you miss it," Griff said firmly. "You think we don't notice." He ran his fingers along Karel's inner arm in a gentle caress. "Sometimes, the way you take hold of things... the way you place items around the flat, not necessarily in a practical place, but in a way that has a certain effect. I can see you imagining how you would put things together, how you would display them for pleasure."

"You touch textures as if you want to taste them. You linger over fabrics and surfaces," Leroy added, nodding at Griff.

"It's in the way you interact with us, too. You take your time, praise everything. See fabulous where we see just ordinary. When you hold us, you run your hands over everything, whether we're clothed or stark naked. And it's not just in your sense of touch—you savour the sweat and the groans and the ways we move..."

Leroy snorted. "I think you even enjoy the mess

we make, because I've seen you take care clearing it up, choosing what's useful, what's beautiful, and what has no potential except to go in the trash."

Oh God, did he? How bloody embarrassing, how needy—

"When was the last time you worked on something?" Leroy asked.

"I'm only an amateur. It's just a hobby."

Griff snorted. "That's not an answer."

When he'd first been in London, Karel had rented a few hours in a local art warehouse and spent time planning installations that he hoped one day to create. It had been a welcome break from his day job, and a salve to his artistic needs. But that had been so many years ago, he'd almost forgotten it.

"I couldn't," he said, slowly. Griff was still stroking his arm. Leroy was breathing more heavily than usual in his ear. "We talked about this before. Leroy, you use the space—"

"Not all of it. And I have use of the dance group's studio now."

"This is your home." But the minute the words left his mouth, Karel realised he would lose this argument. Leroy's eyes sparked even more brightly: Griff's grip tightened as if with an "gotcha!" moment.

"Ah, but it's yours too!" Leroy said smartly. "Or it will be, as soon as you move in properly. Dear Karel..."

"You're here with us. No issue, no doubt." That was Griff's bluntness, as always. "We want to share with you. That includes everything we have."

Karel had never heard anything so naively generous in his life. "I... could pay extra rent for occasional use."

Leroy shrugged. "Why? The flat is all mine, man. Well, my mother's, as you know. But she's happy if I'm happy. If *we're* happy." He linked his arm in Karel's. "Wouldn't this make you happy too?"

Yes, it would make him happy. Ridiculously so. His gaze ranged around the room, drinking in the perfect light, the high ceiling, the space to pace around a model and gain all perspectives. He hadn't expected to have this opportunity for many more years, if at all.

"Do you know what mess I make?" he said, half-jokingly. Was this really going to happen?

"Like we care. So that's settled. Good." Leroy hummed in satisfaction. "Tomorrow you can start moving in your arty bits and bobs—" Griff snorted at him, but he just laughed. "Or whatever it is you use, whatever you need. Why would I know? I'm the dancer, not the artist, remember?"

They laughed, they kissed. Karel was still stunned at the thought of the gift he'd been given—the opportunity he could treasure. Then they sat and cuddled for a long while, mostly in silence. Karel had thought they wanted sex, but although they were all highly charged—on each side he could feel the other men's heightened pulse, through the skin of his arm, his thigh—no one made the first move. They just leaned back against the mirror, settling contentedly with each other.

Karel was almost scared: he thought he wanted to cry.

After a couple of minutes. Griff shifted, and maybe not just to get more comfortable. "Did we bully you to come back here with us, Karel? That first time?"

It was a strange question, even from Griff. "Of course not."

"It's only because we knew at once that we wanted you with us. But maybe we didn't explain ourselves properly."

"You're both confident men," Karel said. "You know what you want, and that shouldn't need over explaining." He hugged them both, though it was a tricky manoeuvre considering the angle of their seating. "You have a strong will."

"Ain't that the truth," Leroy murmured. "But so do you. You're strong. Calm. Determined. Thoughtful."

"Makes us wonder," Griff said. "How *are* you the way you are?"

Karel didn't know what they meant. Maybe he didn't want to seek more deeply.

"Strength is in your whole attitude to life, to work, to love. It's not just about your muscles, though, God knows, I'm pretty keen on them too." Griff chuckled, but Karel suddenly didn't feel the humour.

"I just get along. I do what's needed." The other two were uncharacteristically quiet. What were they asking from him? His gut churned painfully and the prickling in his eyes hadn't let up. "Sometimes you have to draw the reserves from within, and I'm lucky to have them."

"Karel." Leroy's whisper was balm on his throat. "There's no pressure. No judgement."

Griff's soft growl was more of a purr. "We're here for you."

Tell us. That's what they meant.

Words suddenly spilled from Karel, almost

unbidden. "My grandmother's brothers both died in the second world war, in Czechoslovakia as it was then. She saw them shot as presumed traitors. They weren't anything of the sort, but there were a lot of murders in wartime, either to scare dissenters, or in retribution. There was rarely any valid trial—no genuine crime. Just a bullet or a noose." The other men had tensed against him. "Andula—my grandmother—was only a child, and their parents had already died. She was barely a teenager, an orphan left alone with her twin sister, Pavla, without any other family to provide for them. Mama has told us the story many times." His mother had always been honest with Karel and Ada about their family history. She believed strongly that family chronicles must be carried forward, enshrined in memories, if not physical records.

"My great aunt Pavla was always fragile, and the loss of her brothers disturbed her even more. She couldn't be left on her own for too long and, even as a teenager, she couldn't have managed a job. So, my grandmother took casual work where she could find it, and struggled to keep the two of them both alive and well, with only random help from friends and neighbours. It wasn't easy in Czechoslovakia at the end of the war."

Somehow, the twins had survived that poverty-stricken aftermath, and his grandmother had gone on to marry well and happily, with a handful of children, including Karel's mother. And wherever she had gone, whatever family had surrounded her, Andula had always supported her delicate sister. The two women had lived with Karel's family, cared for by Karel's mother, his máma, until they died at a comfortable old age within a year of each other. Karel had been a child at the time, and Ada still a baby. But the continuing tales of the sisters' earlier lives, while shocking, had always allowed him to keep them as part of his family.

Karel's mother had never doubted she should care for her older family, as well as the new generation. Her formative years had been guided by the matriarchal sisters, the consequences of their harsh, early life kept fresh in her memory. She'd ingrained in Karel, Ada, and his other sisters and brother, that such things must constantly be remembered if only to ensure—or at the very least, pray—that they never happened again.

"Mama keeps everything," Karel said. His voice sounded shaky, and a damp trail on his cheek may have been a single tear.

"Karel?" A whisper from Leroy.

"While I was growing up as a child," he continued, his mind now in another time and place, "Mama wouldn't throw out anything, in case it would be useful in the future. Packaging, broken gadgets, clothes we'd outgrown, every letter or card we'd ever received. It drove *táta*, my dad, wild. But that had been her life as a child, her mother and aunt ever frightened of returning to those post-war times, when there was never enough of anything. Mama couldn't shake the habit, even when we were comfortably off. She was still hoarding things, even when the sisters died, even up until the day I flew to the UK. And although she protests against it when I call home, I expect she still is." A gentle smile teased the edges of his mouth. "She knows it's a little obsessive, but she can't stop. And I was glad for it, in many ways—she had always let me use anything in the house to make art. She liked what I did with it. But sometimes... it's difficult to understand her. To connect with her world."

He drew a deep breath. Thoughts of his family, and the history he had left on the other side of Europe, were so often the things that made him over-emotional. Yet tonight? The emotion was almost overwhelming, but it also brought relief and rest. "I've never told anyone about my family history, not here in the UK."

Griff made a soft sound, almost a sob, and hugged closer into Karel's side.

"Griff. Leroy." Karel wanted—needed—to know. "Am I like that, too? Do I hold things back, do I hoard things, to protect myself?"

Leroy gently pulled away so that he could sit straight and look directly into Karel's face. "That's crap, you know it. It's all made you the man you are today, but you're responsible for your own life now, and that's a good place to be in. Everything you do, Karel, reflects your care, your respect. But maybe now we know why you're the way you are. Where your strength of character came from."

This was all too much. Karel didn't know why he felt so vulnerable: by now, he wasn't sure if it was pain or respite he was feeling. All he knew was that he felt temporarily, but horribly adrift. "I don't always want to be strong."

"Jesus, Karel!" Leroy's angry tone startled him. "Don't you think we, of all people, understand that? You've heard me cry in the studio, for God's sake. Haven't you?"

Startled, Karel could see fresh tears in the other man's eyes.

"And taken the knife out of my hand," Griff said

on his other side, so softly. His face was paler than usual.

Karel didn't know what to say. He wanted to believe they were still with him, still loving him, the support could go both ways...

"Let us in," Leroy murmured. "Let out the fear, and let us in."

"You can't scare us," Griff said. "Not if we're all here together. We're changing things, right? And all for the better."

"I want to. I really want to." The words slipped from Karel's mouth, though he couldn't remember forming them.

"So. Relax. Thank you for sharing with me," Leroy said. "With us. I love you." He kissed Karel then, a deep, soft kiss that tangled against Karel's tongue and started his heart racing afresh. The distress inside him eased: the nerves dissolved in warm, physical pleasure. *I'm home.*

"Gotta say, though. Are you moving in now?" Griff urged, his teeth nibbling at the lobe of Karel's ear, which may have been the only part of Karel's body he could reach at that moment. "I mean, seriously. I mean, soon? You don't *have* to, because of, you know, that bullying thing, which I'm not convinced yet you don't think it was—"

"Griff." Leroy warned, yet Griff ignored him.

"But dammit, we're all stupid in love, there's plenty of room for you in the flat, and Leroy can start contributing properly to the bills again now he's earning decent money. Plus, we always let you have the first call on the shower in the morning, and I continue to buy all the ingredients for that dumpling loaf and sauerkraut dish you say you love so much—"

"Don't see *you* refusing seconds," Leroy murmured.

"—whatever the gross pig of a dancer says, as, let's face it, he'd live on that homemade horseradish recipe of yours that you say was your grandmother's—"

"Stop. Stop!" Karel was laughing now, in a real emotional mess, as his body shook with amusement at their bickering, joy at their touch, and amazement at the man he had become in such a short space of time. "I'll move in tomorrow, I promise. I had already decided, but I wasn't sure the offer was still open—"

"Stupid, stupid, it always has been." Leroy was all but crowing with delight. "But right now I don't want to talk about that."

"About anything," Griff added, sliding his hand

under Karel's T-shirt.

"And you're preaching to the converted," Karel gasped.

They rolled back down onto the floor, dragging the throw underneath them. They'd fucked on the blanket many times, either on the bed, or the sofa, or even the living room floor. But this time, whether it was the room they were in, the intense emotions raised among them all, the excited satisfaction of Karel's decision, or a combination of all of it—whatever it was, it lent a new and poignant sensuality to their making out.

Karel pulled Leroy on top of him, who straightened and peeled off his vest with a single, fluid motion. Karel's sight was obscured for a moment while Griff tugged his shirt over his head, then he was back in the action, bare chest against Leroy's. A suddenly nude Griff now knelt at his shoulder, holding his erect cock loosely in one hand so that it nudged damply at Karel's cheek, tantalisingly out of reach to suck, until...

Griff leaned forward, guided Karel's head to the side so they faced each other, then fed his cock firmly through Karel's lips.

Leroy gave a loud moan of arousal, and started wriggling out of his shorts and leggings.

Karel placed an anchoring hand on Griff's fleshy hip while he licked his way up and down the warm, heavy shaft. Griff's taste was always thrilling, as if his volatile moods seasoned his skin, bringing novelty every time. And his vocabulary of sounds gave variety, too. Like now, he groaned and growled and urged Karel on to grip harder, deeper, wetter.

Seated higher than them both, Leroy was straddled across Karel's hips. He shed his clothes and pushed Karel's sweats to down below his knees, so his naked arse bobbed on Karel's lap. A tube of lube appeared in Leroy's hand—where the hell *did* he keep all the accessories stored, and especially here in such a spartan room?—and Karel watched out of the corner of his eye as Leroy reached under his balls to lubricate his hole.

God. Karel wondered if this constant state of excitement was healthy. His dick ached for attention, swelling painfully between his thigh and Leroy's hip, as Leroy rocked on his groin. Then Leroy lifted up on his knees over Karel, steadied himself with a hand on Griff's shoulder, and lowered himself down over Karel's cock.

Karel shouted aloud, albeit muffled by a mouthful of Griff.

"*Fuck!*" Griff gasped, a wealth of excitement in the single word, his gaze darting between Leroy taking Karel inside, and his own cock thrusting in and out of Karel's mouth.

Karel didn't know whether to laugh or cry: he couldn't have articulated anything better himself. He reached his free hand to Leroy's cock, gripping as hard as he dared. He surrendered to the other men's rhythms, Leroy riding him and thrusting in and out of Karel's fist, Griff pumping into Karel's mouth, deeper with each stroke.

The climaxes tumbled from them in confused, delirious, staggered steps. Leroy burst first, yelling and laughing. Sweat trickled from his inner thighs onto Karel's legs, and blobs of his seed dripped onto Karel's pubic hair. No one seemed to care about *this* mess. Griff groaned next, spitting come into Karel's mouth in several spurts. His cock pressed awkwardly against the inside of Karel's cheek, and Karel had to concentrate hard to avoid the scrape of his teeth on Griff's sensitive, post-climax skin. Yet that concentration couldn't be held for long as his own orgasm spiralled up from his groin to his belly.

"Yes." That's what he thought he said, but the actual sound was much more garbled. Griff pulled out of his mouth, squeezing the last drops of his come onto Karel's tongue, but Karel's throat still felt tight, his flesh prickled as if the top layer had been shaved, and his mind was kaleidoscopic rush of desire.

"Yes," Leroy repeated, his gaze on Karel, eager and mischievous, deliberately tightening his anal muscles around Karel's dick.

"Yes," Griff repeated soothingly, still panting from coming, his hand gripping Karel's shoulder as if urging him on.

Karel came with a frantic, moaning mewl that would have embarrassed him in any other time and place. Griff sighed loudly as Karel bucked under his grip, and Leroy shouted with gleeful satisfaction as Karel slammed the last few times up into him.

Who needs words?

Chapter 14

Karel gifted his first completed sculpture project to *With A Kick*. It was based on a trio of copper bowls, which he'd reclaimed from light fittings that Curtis had recovered from the old theatre as he'd promised. They were filled with polished stones of varying sizes but all in the shape of ice cream scoops, mounted in poured acrylic paint that had set hard, and topped with shaved spirals of metal and plastic. Some were of plain, natural colours but he'd also used vibrantly patterned electrical cable in amongst it, like twists of citrus fruit and the crumbled wafers Lee often used in the real life ice creams. It was a fun piece, Karel knew that: it hadn't taken long to make, and he wasn't looking to be presented at the Tate Modern. No, he wanted somehow to show his appreciation for the place that had been his introduction to the friends he'd made in the area. And, indirectly, to his first experiences with Griff and Leroy.

Patrick was astonished and very impressed. Lee made more noise about it, including happy yelps as he praised the piece, and rushed around finding a small, covered table near the front of the café where it could be displayed. But, to Karel, the thoughtful, moved expression on Patrick's face was even more gratifying.

Outside the shop, the street was very busy. Ever since the arts festival had opened, passing trade from the nearby Soho venues had increased exponentially. Also, a group of nearby restaurants and cafes were opening temporary stalls on the pavement to sell snack food for the tourists. It was all good news for local businesses, including *With A Kick*, but Patrick did look a little weary.

When he was invited to stay for a coffee, Karel insisted Patrick joined him. Patrick looked glad of the rest, though he chatted happily and eagerly enough about the festival and the new business. *With A Kick*'s unique and cheekily-named ices had attracted a lot of evening visitors, at the end of their day attending exhibitions and shows.

"I'm glad you called in," Patrick eventually said. "And not just for your gift. Karel, it's really splendid. Witty and fascinating as well as aesthetically beautiful. You are very talented indeed."

Karel dismissed the praise: he wasn't used to it. "What else did you want to talk about? Is it more refurbishment work for the shop?" A lot of the materials Curtis had rescued from the old theatre were stored in a corner of the studio at the flat, and still had plenty of life in them, whether in recycling or in Karel's art. He was full of an anticipatory buzz nowadays, planning and dreaming of creation.

"Actually, I want you to talk to Mr. Amstel."

"Does he need work done on his shop?" Mr Amstel's German grocery was long established, well stocked, and frequented by many loyal customers, but it didn't always display things well enough to tempt new custom. Some of his recipes reminded Karel of old Czech family meals and they'd often chatted about ingredients, mainly for Griff's benefit, as Karel still couldn't do much more than throw a simple stew and pasta together.

"No, he needs a different kind of tradesman."

"For the festival? He's setting up one of the food stalls, isn't he?" Karel was nodding already. He could absorb another new project, as work had temporarily ceased on the hotel job, just while the festival was on. He'd be happy to help out setting up and breaking down the stalls, and maybe would even volunteer to take a shift in the kitchens...

"No. Well, he is, but it's not exactly about that." Patrick was being surprisingly circumspect. "I believe one of your friends is a chef. I wondered if we could call on his expertise for the street?"

Karel was confused. "Don't you already have contacts in the hotel trade?" While *With A Kick* had been closed, Patrick had managed to negotiate the use of a local hotel's freezers, until his own were back in place. "And Nuri's brothers run a restaurant."

Patrick nodded with a quick grimace of frustration. "Of course, yes, they're all involved already. But this is something else. A catering job, at Mr A's store. And I wanted to offer the opportunity to your friend first of all. We would all benefit from his talents, but also... you know. He may like the experience."

He means Griff, Karel suddenly realised. Patrick and Mr Amstel were offering Griff a job, not something permanent or all-consuming, but possibly something Griff could cope with. And do well. Karel knew this was all he ever wanted—his men to do well and be well.

"He's not good in public," he said cautiously, just in case Patrick hadn't remembered how Griff was, even after all the hours Karel must have blathered on about his partners.

"I understand. It would only be for a couple of hours each day until the festival is over, and the kitchen is situated in the back of Mr Amstel's shop, so it's entirely localised. No one else would be allowed in. And there'll be someone else on the stall to take the orders and deal with the public."

Karel could feel the excitement and promise as a physical lump in his throat. "Patrick. I hardly know what to say, it's a marvellous offer. Thank you so much for the thought. But... why Griff?"

"Why not?" Patrick's tone was firm. "I've been thinking about it a lot since we last had the chance to chat properly. Both of your men... well, we all need to feel we belong, don't we?"

A few days later found Karel, Leroy, and Ada at

With A Kick as a busy afternoon slid into a warm, more relaxed evening. Leroy had finished his last performance, for the festival at least, and they were all celebrating with ice cream. Ada was shamelessly slurping up the chocolate flavoured scoop in Top and Tails they'd come to call "Griff's".

She paused and tapped Karel on the shoulder. "*Co je to*, brother? What's up? You keep peering out of the window at Mr A's shop."

Karel shifted awkwardly on his seat. His legs felt itchy, his attention distracted. "I probably need to check things out."

"Again?" Leroy winked at Ada, though his gaze at Karel was fond. "You know, he checks in with Griff all the time. He brings him to the shop, he texts in the middle of the day, then he returns at the end of his work, even before he comes home to change."

Karel grinned ruefully. "More fool, me. He doesn't seem to want the company when I'm there."

"Fool indeed." Leroy frowned at him. "You misunderstand completely. It's because he knows you'll be there, that's why he relaxes."

"That doesn't make sense," Karel said, rather touchily.

"Yes, it does," chorused both Leroy and Ada.

Karel rolled his eyes to the sound of their laughter, pushed back his chair, and wandered across the street to Mr Amstel's grocery.

Tables and chairs had been set out on the pavement, still allowing enough space for pedestrians, and a wooden counter placed over the shop doorway. Normal grocery sales were being restricted to the mornings during the festival, then food sales were started in the afternoon. The stall offered a small selection of dishes to eat outside or take away, and Karel had tried them all so far. The smell of today's choice, Currywurst, was amazingly good and he hoped for a portion of Spatzle on the side, the tasty egg noodles heaped with an oversized pile of cheese.

But firstly, he would check on Griff.

Mr Amstel waved to him from inside the shop and hurried out through the small exit beside the stall. "Karel! Most good to see you." Behind him was Curtis, chewing his way through bratwurst in a bun. He wasn't just there for the food: he was helping most of the food vendors this week with general set up duties. Though if that meant he got fed better than usual, he'd confessed to Karel, who was he to complain?

"How is he doing today?" Karel asked Mr Amstel.

Mr Amstel shrugged. "You ask this every day, right? You are very protective of your friend."

Curtis snorted then hid his mouth behind a napkin.

"All is safe. I show you again," Mr Amstel protested, though he was smiling at the same time. "I have the stall in front of the shop, yes? No one comes in or out apart from me, my family, and Gruff."

"Griff."

Curtis plucked at Karel's sleeve, an ill-concealed grin on his face. "That's just what Mr A calls him. I can't get him to change it. Griff doesn't seem to mind."

"See here." Mr Amstel was determined to show Karel how well he was handling things. "My nephew sells the food, my nieces do the teas and beers."

Beer? Karel opened his mouth to alert Mr—

"But I give Gruff only one beer, he explains that it makes him a little crazy." Mr Amstel chattered on. "I am much the same, but I blame that on my giant heap of assorted medication." He gave a loud, hearty chuckle. "We say I rattle when I walk. Gruff makes up the joke, with my most cheeky niece."

—and Karel shut his mouth again. And smiled.

When he glanced over Mr Amstel's head, he could see Griff working furiously indoors, behind the shop counter. The Amstel family had rigged up a couple of additional hobs to cook on, and Griff was juggling and stirring up to four deep pans at once. Two young girls and an even younger-looking boy darted around with foil containers and cutlery: as soon as Griff had finished a batch of the wurst and noodles, they scooped it into the containers and bussed it swiftly out to the shop front where Mr Amstel's considerably older and rather bossy—in Karel's opinion—nephew sold it to the passing visitors.

"He's bossy, isn't he?" Mr Amstel was proving as alarmingly perceptive as so many other friends had been recently. "But he is making the sales very well. And that means more money for the business and my niece."

"Your niece?"

"She is actress," Mr Amstel said proudly. "One day, movie star."

"*This* day, stage school membership fees," Curtis murmured on Karel's other side.

"That's brilliant," Karel said to Mr A, though he was distracted. He was watching Griff as he gestured imperiously to one of the girls to pass him something or other. He waved the spoon so vigorously it slipped from his fingers but, darting to his side, she caught it deftly, and stuck out her tongue at him. Griff frowned.

Karel held his breath.

And then Griff burst into loud laughter. Karel could hear it, even from out here on the street. He mussed the girl's hair fondly, though she wriggled away in mock disgust. Then he turned to answer a query from the little boy, bending to the youngster's height. Karel could see Griff's face more clearly from this angle. He'd pushed his glasses up onto his head and his eyes shone, he had a blotch of golden-tinted ketchup on his cheek, and he was speaking earnestly to the boy, as if to a fellow adult.

"They like Gruff," Mr Amstel said quietly, breaking into his thoughts. "And he likes to be with them. Each day, he stays a little longer. We are finding many new recipes. I have never known anyone master a cuisine so quickly, so well."

"He's marvellous," Karel said. "He's so talented. He deserves this." His gaze returned to Griff, who hadn't yet realised Karel was there.

Mr Amstel cleared his throat politely.

"What?" Karel asked. When he looked

quizzically back at Mr A, the old man winked at him.

"You want to go and talk to him?"

"No," Karel said quietly. He watched Griff twisting between work surfaces, chopping ingredients, calling encouragement to the young Amstels, laughing and joking with them. "I'll catch up with him later."

Mr Amstel nodded with satisfaction, and patted Karel on the shoulder. "The three of you must need much food to keep so fit," he said, without any irony that Karel could detect. "I will give him extra portions to take home tonight!"

Chapter 15

They were all still on the street when the final festival stalls broke up. It was past eleven o'clock, and the temporary licences were at an end for the day. Patrick had kept *With A Kick* open, and Lee and Phiz carried a few chairs and tables onto the pavement under the awning. The ice cream and coffee for friends were free.

To Karel's surprise and delight, Griff didn't ask to go home immediately, but joined them at a café table.

"It's the last week of the festival," Ada said. She'd already opened one of Mr Amstel's containers and was greedily forking her way through one of her brother's dinner portions. "I'll miss all this excitement."

"We'll still be dancing," Leroy said, and the pair

of them grinned at each other like conspirators. "And you can come to all my regular performances."

"At Master Mac's as well?" Ada asked mischievously. "Will you still dance there?"

"Sometimes." Leroy nodded and flicked a glance at Karel. "I like it there, and I have a special audience to please."

"Well, I can't pretend I understand how you all manage living together, though my little brother certainly looks good on it," Ada said, blithely, unaware of Karel's embarrassed grimace, "But I love the way you all *work* together. And this food is fabulous, Griff." Ada's praise was rather spoiled by her spitting pasta onto the table—eating and talking at the same time had never been her forte—but Griff blushed nonetheless. "A street food supremo, eh? Someone told me your foster family are coming into London to try out the food this week, is that right?"

Griff tried to shrug nonchalantly, but couldn't hide the look of stunned delight in his eyes. Leroy reached out a hand and squeezed his tightly.

Ada smiled warmly at Griff. Most of her interaction had been with Leroy, in their dance sessions, but she and Griff had bonded over food several times already. She inelegantly waved her fork at him, sending a spray of curry sauce into the remains of Karel's bowl of ice cream. "You've been hiding your lights under a proverbial bushel, my good man. Hope you're going to continue catering to the hungry masses."

Karel and Leroy glanced quickly at each other.

But Griff didn't even pause before replying. "Too right, I am! Mr A and I have been making plans. We're gonna set up a monthly food stall here in the street. The Chinese restaurant and grocer wants in, and Nuri's brothers will provide some sample Turkish cuisine. Curtis will help us get the ingredients at trade rates, and Bryan—Phiz's boyfriend, you know him?—will help with trade licences. It'll help sell the *With A Kick* menu, too. I can promote it through the blog."

Karel stared, fascinated. Social enthusiasm was a new side of Griff for him.

Griff returned a quick, almost furtive look at Karel. "Not like I'll be any kind of entrepreneur."

"Not overnight, no." Karel smiled to soften the words and brushed his hand over Griff's. "But give it a few months."

Leroy snorted happily into the long, ice cream-topped latte in front of him. "Branson does bratwurst, right?"

"Moron," Griff snapped at Leroy quite cheerily.

"Double-moron," Leroy replied smartly, though new insults had obviously escaped him.

"Mr A can't pay me," Griff said quickly to Karel. "I mean, he'll be spending out for the ingredients—but he's offered me a profit share."

"Excellent strategy," said Ada, her covetous gaze on Leroy's latte now.

"So, you'll be earning," Karel said to Griff with pleasure. *In the outside world.*

"Yeah. Whoa." Griff flushed. "Pretty weird feeling for me, right?"

"Contributing to the home!" Leroy announced.

"To the family," Karel said, more softly so that maybe only his men heard.

They stayed for a while longer, until Ada left to catch a train home, and Patrick wanted to close up the shop. Griff was still excited and happy, but Karel could see the restlessness in his hands that meant he was starting to get anxious.

"Karel?" Leroy was at his side, an arm already around Griff. Of course, he would know the signs too.

"We'll get a cab," Karel said firmly. Nuri had left him his card for whenever they needed a ride home in his taxi. "So many things to celebrate, we deserve the luxury, right?"

As they lingered on the pavement, waiting for the taxi, a guy walked past, did a double-take, and then paused in front of Karel. He was reasonably good-looking, well built, and well dressed in smart jeans and jacket, but there was an ugly twist to his mouth that Karel took an immediate dislike to.

"Leroy? Hey there. Griff, too."

Leroy's eyes hardened. "Tod."

The guy leaned forward, leering over them both. "So. Haven't seen you for a while. Who's the new guy?"

For a moment, it looked as if Leroy wouldn't answer, and Griff had somehow shrunk up to Karel's side like a human limpet.

"This is Karel," Leroy said eventually. "He's with us."

Tod's beady gaze darted between the three of them. "You mean, travelling with you? Or staying with you?"

"He lives with us," Griff burst out.

Karel felt the very briefest tightening in his chest

and then he relaxed into it. "Yes, I live with Griff and Leroy." It was actually very easy to say, and becoming just as easy to believe.

Tod looked both confused and aggrieved. His gaze narrowed onto Karel, like the others weren't even there. "Well, fuck me. They never invited me to stay over for breakfast, let alone enough time to get my fucking shoes under the table. What did you do to deserve that, eh?"

His gaze ran over Karel, blatant, lascivious, downright creepy. All it needed was for him to lick his lips and Karel would have felt violated without a single touch.

"Maybe I can see that for myself," Tod said, nodding with satisfaction, his tone snide. "Now *you*... You're just my type."

"And what type is that?" Karel all but snarled back. "Anyone who has a *dick*?"

Griff gave a surprised grunt—Karel was rarely rude—and Leroy tightened his hand on Karel's elbow. Did he think Karel was going to take a swing for this tosser? Karel admitted he was sorely tempted. The day had been good, the happiness high, and he'd thought he was a usually level-headed guy.

Until now.

Tod was only briefly fazed. "Just surprised, that's all. These guys were never really a safe bet, you know?"

"No," Karel said, conscious that his voice had deepened, coarsened. "I don't know."

It appeared he'd also moved forward, because Tod's eyes widened and he took a hurried step back, nearly tumbling off the kerb. "Hey. No need to get rough, man. They're just guys. I mean, we're all players." He swallowed quickly, his gaze on Karel's shoulders, Karel's tight biceps, Karel's firm glare. "Fucking fuss for nothing. I mean... Fuck me."

"No," Karel repeated. "Most definitely, no."

Tod started backing away across the street, speaking more quickly. "Whatever. You change your mind, find me at the club. You'll be back there soon, I guess. Depends who gets tired of who first, right?" A taxi pulled up behind him—luckily it wasn't Nuri, who was on his way from another fare—and Tod quickly swaggered over to climb in. The slam of the door, the tick-tick of the vehicle engine, and he was gone from view.

Back on the pavement, there was an uncomfortably long moment of silence.

Then Leroy let out a breath. "Fuck. Jesus. That arrogant shit. Never thought we'd come across him again."

"Yeah. Ugh," Griff said, but his voice was shaky. They glanced at each other, then at Karel.

Karel stared back at them. Waiting.

"I mean," Leroy said, talking to Karel, but now apparently fascinated by the random graffiti on a shop's shutter across the street. "He obviously liked *you*."

Griff bit his lower lip, his expression fierce in a way Karel didn't immediately understand. "And hey. You know. He has a big dick."

"What the hell... Didn't you hear what I said to him?" Karel couldn't believe this. "You think I want to take him up on his offer?"

Leroy flushed deeply. His hands were clenched into fists, the veins in his forearms sharply defined. "If you don't want to be exclusive, that's okay. You can have other men if you want, we'd understand, so if you wanna try him—"

"What? Like an ice cream? Try him out like a new flavour?" Karel startled himself with the sudden roar in his voice. "Who the hell do you think I am? Do you really think I'm like that? *Do you?*"

"Oh God," Leroy said weakly. He started shaking his head nonsensically. "Oh fuck. What am I saying? Oh *fuck*."

"Wait. Karel!" Griff's voice was even louder than Karel's. "No, we don't think you're like that. No way. And yes, you can have other men, but—shit! I don't want that, not with you, not without you. I mean, basically, Leroy's a fucking supremely, stupid arse—"

"Oh Jesus, yes, I am, he's right—" Leroy's eyes were anguished, his pupils blown, his breath shallow.

"—because we *wouldn't* understand, actually, would we, Leroy?"

"No. Oh God, no. I wouldn't. *We* wouldn't." Leroy was struggling to get himself back under control. "I want you. You and Griff. No one else. I don't know what the hell I meant, saying that stuff about not being exclusive. It's *not* okay with me, or Griff."

Griff was frowning angrily at Leroy, though his voice wobbled. "Yeah. I mean, no. No way, you arse."

"It's just..."

"Just *what*?" Karel almost growled.

"I'm fucking scared you'll leave," Leroy whispered.

"When you get a better offer," Griff added, voice

still shaky.

Karel almost bit through his tongue trying not to yell at the two of them. "Like *Tod*, you mean?"

"God. Not *him*. Please? He was a shit." Griff sounded desperate. "We only played for one evening, then couldn't wait to see the back of him."

Leroy's shaking head turned to nodding, just as vigorously. "*Christ*, but I've made some mistakes with men, you know?"

"We both have. Don't hold it against us. You deserve a hell of a sight better." Griff blinked fiercely. It set up little shivers of reflection in his glasses. "And he *doesn't* have a big dick, right? I just said that. I don't know why the fuck I did."

"Neither do I." Leroy moaned, and punched Griff's arm.

"I do that sort of crazy shit all the time." Griff gabbled on. "I don't deserve decent men. You can have whoever you like, Karel, I mean, maybe you should dump *me* but keep up with Leroy—"

"Shut up! Shut the hell up, both of you!"

There was another sudden, shocked silence. Karel was profoundly glad that all their friends and family had gone home. He didn't care about disturbing the late-night passers-by, but he *did* care about loved ones seeing how he couldn't keep his men in order: couldn't, apparently, keep them centred.

"This stops right now," he said, his voice husky with emotion. "No more showing off, no more lies, no more stupid, out of the blue, totally unnecessary fears." He gentled his voice with an effort. "I'm not leaving, but I also can't take the games. I don't want other men, I don't want to split you two up, I don't want to go, or argue, or beat up anyone. Except maybe that tosser who upset you both so much and who doesn't deserve any guy he's going to treat like that."

"Told you at the time he'd be a wanker," Griff half-whispered to Leroy, who punched him back in the arm again.

"I'm not looking anywhere else," Karel said. He almost spit out the words, the idea offended him that much. "Nor for anyone else. I'm with you. And that's what I want. *All* I want. I want us to be together. If that's too difficult for you to understand or accept, now is the time to say. We can go our different ways without any blame or hard feelings. But it's the last thing *I* want."

Leroy drew himself up. His eyes were too bright, but his jaw jutted with determination. "It's the last thing I want, too."

Griff just nodded dumbly.

Karel sighed. "So why the hell do you keep questioning it? It's the same as calling me a liar, and I won't have that. If I'm unhappy or angry about something, I will say so. If I think one of us is making the others unhappy, I'll say something about that too."

"Oh fuck." This time, it was more of a sigh from Leroy.

"Yeah. Fuck," Griff repeated, blinking hard. "And not in a good way, right?"

And then... Karel laughed. "You're like bloody bookends," he said. "Stupid sometimes, but always cute. I love you so much." As they stared at him in startled delight, he scooped them into a hug and kissed both of them on the mouth. With lots of tongue.

Across the street, another taxi had pulled up and was idling with its For Hire light off. Nuri was waiting for them.

"Let's go home," Leroy said, rather breathlessly.

"Gets my vote. We can go for that fuck thing, but in a good way this time, right?" Griff chuckled as he crossed the road, opening the taxi door to greet Nuri and then clambering across the seat.

Karel turned to Leroy as they were both

climbing in after him, a smile still on his lips. "Have you really never invited someone to stay before?"

Leroy flushed, rolled his eyes and, this time, punched Karel in the arm. "Now you're just fishing, man!"

Epilogue

Three months later

Karel stretched up from the framework on the floor of his studio with a weary huff. He needed to bring in one of the tables from the living room and elevate this stage of the project. Working on the base took its toll on his shoulders and lower back.

A pair of hands slid over his shoulders and squeezed hard. That felt pretty damned good on his muscles. So did Leroy's knee nudging the back of his leg, and the smell of Leroy's cologne in his nostrils.

"Need a massage tonight?" Leroy murmured.

"Need it every night," Karel replied with a low

laugh. Leroy was working regularly at the dance studio now, including tutor sessions, and a sideline in learning massage techniques. Karel had moved past the busiest stage of the hotel project—so he could spend more time at home with his art—but he often missed the physically harder work, for keeping his physique loose and in shape.

Leroy perched his chin on Karel's shoulder and looked down Karel's chest to the structure on the floor. "It's wonderful."

"Huh. You don't know what it is."

"So?"

Karel smiled, enjoying the warmth of Leroy's body pressed against his back. "I don't mean to be rude. It's just... I haven't quite finished it yet. It must look like nothing more than raw metal and cloth."

Leroy stepped away and walked slowly around it, his bare feet light on the wooden floor. Karel tried to see it from another man's point of view. He'd built the base from half a reclaimed copper pipe—it was his favourite metal to use, he loved its colour and the way it could glimmer, polished, against other materials. Then a slender, elegantly twisted piece of iron moulding from an old candlestick reared up from its centre, draped with velvet from the theatre curtains, the fabric falling in loose, sensuous folds yet heavy with gold brocade at its hem. Around the base of the moulding and nestling against the edges of the copper base were long strips of cloth, interwoven tightly but boldly matched—rich chocolate-coloured furred fabric with vivid green satin, pale hessian with ridiculously scarlet feathers from an old costume boa.

It made Karel smile, but that was because he knew what it represented to him. It made him ache sadly, too—it was an artist's lot to doubt he could ever communicate his inner vision to a more public view.

Leroy stood in front of him, arms folded across his slender, muscular chest. He clicked his tongue and shook his head. "You think, because it's not a specific shape, I can't find it wonderful?"

"No, I didn't mean that."

"But... I think you did. You think you have to produce something that pleases people, that connects with them. Yeah, that's great, but that's not what it's about really. You're a simple man, Karel. No, not simple intellectually!" Leroy held his hand up to stave off the implied insult. "You feel things strongly and clearly. You've surely learned, however, that others don't respond the same way."

Karel stared at him.

"I do understand, you see," Leroy said softly. "Both I and Griff do. We're both odd characters, not comfortably in a common niche. We both know the difficulty of expressing who and what we are, of building relationships when neither of us is particularly adept at it."

"That's not true. You're both very confident, successful men, at least now you've put your efforts into it. Unique, yes, but you've made your way in the world." Leroy was a rising young star at the dance group, and developing into a fine tutor. Griff was still happier at home, but his pop-up food stall was so successful he was considering running it two days a month rather than just one. And, to his mixed ecstasy and horror, his blog had been mentioned positively on satellite TV channels a couple of times.

Leroy shrugged. The easy, lazy, graceful movement had Karel's cock filling as quickly as it ever did. "Let's say... we were lost, back then. Before you came. I've always hidden behind my dance, expecting others to feel the same swell of joy and expression that I do, expecting it to declare who I am to all and sundry, but without actually having to commit to it publicly. And Griff... just hid from everything. When we two found each other, it was like coming home. A shorthand for a relationship. We understood each other on a much more basic level than other methods of communication."

"Yet you still argue like kids," Karel said.

"Yes." Leroy laughed a little sadly. "And misunderstand. Of course we do. That's life. But we've always stayed together regardless, because at heart we are bound to each other. Because we love each other, and, anyway..."

He couldn't seem to complete the sentence. Suddenly, Karel knew why.

"And because you didn't think anyone else would."

Griff appeared at the open doorway, his expression bemused. He held a pastry tin in one hand and wiped the other one aimlessly down the front of his apron. "Um. Guys. Something up?"

It was as if he'd known he was needed in the room.

Karel held out his hands and both of them came to him. Karel kissed the top of Griff's head, tasting stray puffs of flour. He caressed Leroy's back, touching the sweat of another punishing rehearsal session. And they all made out, sloppily, laughing softly, promising the world with kisses and caresses, but knowing they'd wait to deliver on that promise until they were all in bed together. The passion was always there, but maybe, nowadays, not the panic.

"Leroy's been talking crap again," Karel said.

"That shit about thinking no one would love us, so we made the best of each other instead?" Griff snorted.

"That's how we were," Leroy protested.

Griff leaned into Karel, and nodded. "Yeah. That's how we were."

"Until you joined us," Leroy whispered.

Karel's heart twisted. "Well, like I said, that's crap, isn't it? Because that's changed. Because someone does love you. *I* do. I love you both."

"Thank fuck," Griff said with gusto. "So I won't need to hide your van keys to keep you here as my sex slave."

Leroy chuckled, his face lifted to Karel's for another kiss. "Man, sometimes I think you're the only one who could."

"Or would," Griff added. "Bloody saviour, you are."

"I don't think so." Karel smiled. "Or, let's say that goes both ways." They'd saved him: they'd given him the life and family he craved. Oh... and the mindblowing sex sessions, too. "Besides, you aren't lost like that anymore."

"Yeah. Well. We didn't say we weren't getting better at living in the real world, did we?" said Leroy slyly.

"Enough, now." Karel laughed and pushed them carefully to one side. "I must work. I'm due back on site on Monday, so I want to spend as much time on this as I can, while I'm free." He glanced down at the new structure again. "And maybe you're right— I shouldn't keep worrying about it being understood."

"You like it?" Griff asked. His nose wrinkled as he examined the sculpture, and his eyes were very sharp. "I mean, *you're* satisfied with it?"

"I will be," Karel replied. Yes. He would be. *Of course.* His heart seemed to ease. His opinion of the structure opened out from potential catalogue view to something that spoke to his deepest emotions and made his toes curl with pleasure.

And why hadn't he realised before, that was the best view of all?

"You've got to think of yourself, man," Leroy said. "Not just us, not just others. Not just what's expected of you. And create what you want. Yeah, we're gonna love it, because we love you and you're hot as all hell, but even if someone doesn't—"

"Fuck 'em," Griff said cheerfully.

Leroy rolled his eyes and pushed Griff back towards the door. "No, you arse. I meant, it's the art that matters to Karel. The growth, the struggle, the fulfilment."

Yes, Karel thought. *Yes.*

"You sure that's not the sex slave scenario?" Griff was saying as they paused just outside in the hallway. "Sounds a hell of a lot like it."

Leroy peered briefly back into the studio. "And I say it's wonderful."

Karel grinned, stooping to pick up a roll of purple electrical wire he was going to use to bind the elements into a more cohesive whole.

"It's us, right?" Griff said abruptly, his voice carrying clearly across the room.

Karel stilled, his heart beating too fast. He slowly turned to face them, both standing in the doorway.

"The sculpture. The latest project." Griff waved his hand at it. "There's Leroy, all tall, sinewy, and swathed in sexiness, like the velvet. Me, all furred and pillowy, bold, bright colours, right in-yer-face. And you..."

"The base," Leroy finished. "Smart, polished, strong, a rock beneath us, holding us all three together."

"Yeah," Griff snorted. "Like I said. Sex slave scenario, for definite."

Karel watched and listened as they both ambled away down the hallway out of sight, bickering softly, planning the next meal, wondering what to watch on TV that night. And nowadays, always considering all three of them.

He gazed over the trio of elements in his work—the elegance and vitality, the comfort and cosiness. And lying underneath, the shimmering solidity of a genuine foundation. Leroy, Griff and Karel himself—absorbed by the others, supporting them, savouring their different sensualities, and belonging to and within it all.

He hadn't finished it yet. Who knew how it'd develop over the hours he still had to spend on it? Who knew what it'd come to be?

Looked like *they* did.

He bent over the sculpture again, starting to secure it with the wire. Maybe it'd be finished quicker than he'd planned.

He couldn't help grinning to himself, thinking he might turn in for bed earlier than usual.

About Clare London

For an up to date list of all Clare London's books
please visit http://www.clarelondon.com

Clare London took her pen name from the city
where she lives, loves, and writes. A lone, brave
female in a frenetic, testosterone-fuelled family
home, she juggles her writing with her other day
job as an accountant.

She's written in many genres and across many
settings, with award-winning novels and short
stories published both online and in print. She says
she likes variety in her writing while friends say
she's just fickle, but as long as both theories spawn
good fiction, she's happy. Most of her work features
male/male romance and drama with a healthy
serving of physical passion, as she enjoys both
reading and writing about strong, sympathetic, and
sexy characters.

Clare loves to hear from readers, and you can
contact her at all her social media.

Website + blog: http://www.clarelondon.com

E-mail: clarelondon11@yahoo.co.uk

Newsletter: http://eepurl.com/dv7Pl9

Facebook:
https://www.facebook.com/clarelondonauthor

Twitter: https://twitter.com/clare_london

Goodreads:
http://www.goodreads.com/clarelondon

Amazon:
http://www.amazon.com/author/clarelondon/

Bookbub: https://www.bookbub.com/profile/clare-london

GooglePlay:
https://play.google.com/store/books/author?id=Clare+London

About With A Kick

A new and enticing ice cream franchise, with a unique blend of full flavour, mischief and romance. Patrick and Lee are struggling to make a success of their alcoholic ice cream shop in the centre of tourist London. At the same time, their business partnership may take a turn towards the personal – if either of them can find the time and nerve to go for it! Meanwhile, they cater to the wild and wonderful range of customers in the area, many of whom have their own romantic agenda. Will ice cream be the final ingredient they're all looking for?

A joint-authored project with Sue Brown, this series of romantic novellas are each between 25,000 to 50,000 words and available in e-book.
(P) Also available in print.
The two Collections listed below are also available in audio, narrated by the talented Joel Leslie.
Cover art by Lou Harper.

List and order of titles:

#1 A Twist and Two Balls – Clare London (P)

#2 Hissed as a Newt – Sue Brown

#3 Slap and Tickle – Clare London (P)

#4 Bells and Balls – Sue Brown

#5 Pluck and Play – Clare London (P)

#6 Nice and Snow – Clare London

#7 Smack Happy – Clare London

#8 Double Scoop – Clare London (P)

#9 Top and Tails – Clare London (P)

With A Kick Collection No. 1:
Including #1, #3, #6, #7.

With A Kick Collection No. 2: Including #5, #8.

Clare London - Bibliography

N = Novel / V = Novella

Other titles are short stories

P = also in print

T = also in other language translations

A = also in audio

AT DREAMSPINNER PRESS:

72 Hours (N) (P) (T) (A)

Branded (N) (P)

Compulsion (N) (P)

Sparks Fly (N) (P)

Dancing Days (V)

Footprints (V)

Just-You Eyes (V)

Timeslip (V)

Touch (V)

Bite Night

Charlie Chuckles

One Night Stand

Pop-Ups

The Right Choice

Then and Now

The Peppermint Schnapps Predicament

Wishing on a Blue Star (Anthology)

7&7 (Anthology)

DREAMSPUN DESIRES (all N/P/A)

#19 – Romancing the Wrong Twin

#36 – Romancing the Ugly Duckling

#71 - Romancing the Undercover Millionaire

LONDON LADS (all V)

Chase the Ace (T) (A)

How the Other Half Lives

A Good Neighbour

Peepshow

Between a Rock and a Hard Place

London Lads (Anthology of #1-5) (P)

TRUE COLORS

True Colors (N) (P)

Ambush

Payback

Switch

Flying Colors (N) (P)

AT JOCULAR PRESS (self-published):

Sweet Summer Sweat (N) (P)

Flashbulb (V)

Dear Alex (V)

Out of Time

Muse

Telltale

Limbo

Chat Line

Upwardly Mobile

Say a Little Prayer

Home Sweet Home

Lucky Dip

Secret Santa

Short 'n Sweet – Closet Exhibitionist

Short 'n Sweet – Twelfth Night

WITH A KICK

#1 A Twist and Two Balls (P)

#3 Slap and Tickle (P)

#5 Pluck and Play (P)

#6 Nice and Snow

#7 Smack Happy

#8 Double Scoop (P)

Collection No 1 (#1, #3, #6, #7) (A)

Collection No 2 (#5, #8) (A)

#9 Top and Tails

BOYS IN...

Boys in Brief

Boys in Season

Boys in Hand

AT JCP BOOKS:
Bittersweet Candy Kisses (anthology) (P)

AT CARINA PRESS:
Blinded by Our Eyes (A)
The Tourist

AT JMS BOOKS:
His Gift
What Not to Wear
Dish of the Day
Perfection
The Mask
Nowhere to Hide
Threadbare
Precious Possession
That's Entertainment!
Santa, Actually
Just Like the Movies FREE
Making Camp FREE
Tea and Crumpet (anthology) (P)
Lashings of Sauce (anthology) (P)
British Flash (anthology) FREE

AT PINK SQUIRREL PRESS (self-published):

Winter Warmers (anthology)

Summer Lovin' (anthology)

AT MLR PRESS:

I Do! (anthology) (P)

Illustrated Men (anthology) (P)

44908379R00157

Printed in Poland
by Amazon Fulfillment
Poland Sp. z o.o., Wrocław